# Man of Violence

Bronco Hammer

First Edition

**ISBN: 978-1-892798-31-2**

**Notice**

Consultants and advisors:
Literature and guns - Jeff Trapp, Randy Lewis, Tim Fife, Mike Ratke
Guns and Cigars – Jeff Trapp, Carlo DeBlasio
Musical director – Raven Douglas
Automotive - Mike Cocchiola, Tim Fife
Models – Mike Cocchiola, Jeff Trapp, and some random super model

Bronco Hammer Books are sponsored by
*Tony Chamberlain Super Model Repellent*
Preventing those pesky super models from bothering you while you are trying to
do stuff, like working on your car or cleaning your firearms *(results may vary)*

Consultants and advisors are super geniuses who answered some questions
for me. They are not responsible or accountable for the contents of this book or
related materials. The Genius stuff is to their credit, any errors are mine to own.

# MAN OF VIOLENCE

*"If I advance, follow me.*
*If I retreat, kill me.*
*If I die, avenge me."*
Henri de la Rochejaquelein - Not a puss

*"Fast is fine, but accuracy is everything.*
*In a gun fight... You need to take your time in a hurry."*
Wyatt Earp – Not a puss

*Once we have a war there is only one thing to do. It must be won. For defeat brings worse things than any that can ever happen in war.*
Ernest Hemingway – Not a puss

*A man of violence suffers a nagging question he must have answered.*
Bronco Hammer – Not even close to being a puss

# TABLE OF AWESOME CONTENTS

**TRIGGER WARNINGS** .................................................................. **8**

**PRE-READ BRIEFING** ............................................................. **14**

**CHAPTER 1 – NEVER PISS OFF AN OLD MAN WITH A GUN..... 16**

SEVEN MILE BEACH - OFFICE TOWER, GRAND CAYMAN ................... 16

**CHAPTER 2 – NEVER PISS OFF A PRESIDENT WITH A GUN ..... 27**

PALM BEACH, FLORIDA - THREE DAYS LATER ................................. 27

**CHAPTER 3 – NEVER PISS OFF A RICH KID WITH A GUN......... 43**

CORONADO, CALIFORNIA - THE PRESIDENT'S SECRET ESTATE ............ 43

**CHAPTER 4 – NEVER PISS OFF A COMMIE WITH A GUN......... 55**

THE GREAT HALL OF THE PEOPLE – BEIJING, CHINA ......................... 55
DOWNTOWN LOS ANGELES ......................................................... 61
THE GREAT HALL OF THE PEOPLE – BEIJING, CHINA ......................... 69
HAWAII – FEATHERSTON ESTATE ON THE BIG ISLAND ...................... 72
SURFSIDE - CORONADO, CALIFORNIA ........................................... 75

**CHAPTER 5 – NEVER PISS OFF A SPY WITH A GUN................. 76**

THE TOWER RESORT HOTEL - HAWAII............................................. 76
WASHINGTON, DC..................................................................... 80
THE TOWER OF KONA RESORT HOTEL- HAWAII .............................. 82
NIGHTFALL IN HAWAII ............................................................... 85
FEATHERSTON ESTATE – HAWAII - INSIDE THE MAIN HOUSE ............. 87
FEATHERSTON ESTATE - THE MAIN GATE ...................................... 88
FEATHERSTON ESTATE - INSIDE THE MAIN HOUSE .......................... 89
FEATHERSTON ESTATE GROUNDS ................................................ 91

**CHAPTER 6 – NEVER PISS OFF AN UNSUPERVISED SENIOR CITIZEN WITH A GUN......................................................... 96**

FEATHERSTON ESTATE - HAWAII .................................................. 96
LAKE TEKAPO - SOUTH ISLAND, GOLDBURN'S NEW ZEALAND ESTATE.. 99

FEATHERSTON ESTATE - HAWAII ................................................ 101
WASHINGTON DC................................................................ 111

## CHAPTER 7 – NEVER PISS OFF AN ASSHOLE WITH A GUN.....113

WASHINGTON DC................................................................ 113
NEW YORK CITY – CNT WORLD NEWS BROADCASTING ................. 118
LAKE TEKAPO - SOUTH ISLAND, NEW ZEALAND HILLSIDE ................. 120
BEIJING CHINA ........................................................................ 121
WASHINGTON D.C................................................................ 122
LAKE TEKAPO - SOUTH ISLAND, NEW ZEALAND ESTATE ................. 123
LAKE TEKAPO - SOUTH ISLAND, THE RIDGELINE ABOVE THE NEW ZEALAND
ESTATE ................................................................................ 124
MANILA, PHILIPPINES ............................................................. 126
LAKE TEKAPO - SOUTH ISLAND, NEW ZEALAND ESTATE ................. 130
THE TOWER RESORT HOTEL - CENTURY CITY – MANILA, PHILIPPINES 133
SOUTH ISLAND, NEW ZEALAND – TWO DAYS LATER ...................... 139

## CHAPTER 8 – NEVER PISS OFF A BURMESE WITH A GUN......142

LAKE TEKAPO - SOUTH ISLAND, NEW ZEALAND ESTATE ................. 142
LAKE TEKAPO - SOUTH ISLAND, NEW ZEALAND - RIDGELINE ............ 144
WASHINGTON D.C................................................................ 146
LAKE TEKAPO - SOUTH ISLAND, NEW ZEALAND – RIDGELINE .......... 148

## CHAPTER 9 – NEVER PISS OFF A MARINE WITH A GUN ........156

THE GREAT HALL OF THE PEOPLE - BEIJING ................................. 156
NEW YORK CITY – CNT WORLD NEWS BROADCASTING ................. 157
THE TOWER RESORT HOTEL - CENTURY CITY – MANILA, PHILIPPINES 158
THE TOWER RESORT HOTEL - HONOLULU .................................... 160
TOWER RESORT HOTEL – MANILA, PHILIPPINES............................ 162
NINOY AQUINO INTERNATIONAL AIRPORT – MANILA, PHILLIPPINES.. 165
LANGLEY, VIRGINIA ................................................................ 167
THE TOWER RESORT – MANILLA, PHILIPPINES ............................. 172

## CHAPTER 10 – NEVER PISS OFF A MERCENARY WITH A GUN174

WHITE HOUSE - WASHINGTON DC ............................................ 174
FBI HEADQUARTERS - WASHINGTON DC...................................... 177
THE TOWER RESORT HOTEL – BANGKOK, THAILAND...................... 182
TEA PLANTATION - CHIANG RAI, THAILAND ................................. 186

THE WHITE HOUSE ................................................. 189

BANGKOK, THAILAND ............................................. 190

ZHAO'S QUARTERS - THE GREAT HALL OF THE PEOPLE - BEIJING ...... 195

TEA PLANTATION - CHIANG RAI, THAILAND .................................. 196

IN A HELICOPTER OVER NORTHERN THAILAND ............................. 197

WHITE HOUSE, WASHINGTON DC ............................................ 198

**CHAPTER 11 – NEVER PISS OFF A LADY WITH A GUN .......... 204**

TEA PLANTATION - CHIANG RAI, THAILAND .................................. 204

WASHINGTON DC................................................................. 205

TEA PLANTATION - CHIANG RAI, THAILAND .................................. 206

ZHAO'S QUARTERS - THE GREAT HALL OF THE PEOPLE - BEIJING ...... 211

TEA PLANTATION – CHIANG RAI, THAILAND .................................. 213

EAST VALLEY – OUTER PERIMETER OF THE TEA PLANTATION - CHIANG
RAI, THAILAND ................................................................. 215

WEST VALLEY – OUTER PERIMETER OF THE TEA PLANTATION - CHIANG
RAI, THAILAND ................................................................. 219

EAST VALLEY – PERIMETER OF THE TEA PLANTATION - CHIANG RAI,
THAILAND ....................................................................... 225

WEST VALLEY - – PERIMETER OF TEA PLANTATION - CHIANG RAI,
THAILAND ....................................................................... 226

OFFICE OF THE DIRECTOR OF CENTRAL INTELLIGENCE ..................... 231

NORTH SIDE - INNER-PERIMETER OF THE TEA PLANTATION MANSION -
CHIANG RAI, THAILAND ...................................................... 234

THE WHITE HOUSE – WASHINGTON DC ..................................... 235

THE GREAT HALL OF THE PEOPLE - BEIJING .................................. 236

TEA PLANTATION MANSION - CHIANG RAI, THAILAND..................... 238

TEA PLANTATION - CHIANG RAI, THAILAND – BEYOND THE INNER
PERIMETER ..................................................................... 239

THE WHITE HOUSE – OVAL OFFICE ........................................... 244

JUNGLE OUTSIDE OF CHIANG RAI, THAILAND ............................... 246

**CHAPTER 12 - NEVER PISS OFF AN AMERICAN WITH A GUN 249**

THE GREAT HALL OF THE PEOPLE - BEIJING .................................. 254

BIO-WEAPON LAB - BAJA CALIFORNIA ....................................... 255

CORPORATE JET – OVER THE PACIFIC OCEAN ............................... 257

**CHAPTER 13 - NEVER PISS OFF MCCARTNEY AND FALCONE WITH A GUN** ...................................................................**263**

    BAJA, MEXICO ........................................................................ 263

    THE WHITE HOUSE - WASHINGTON DC ..................................... 265

    BAJA, MEXICO ........................................................................ 266

    COVERT BIOWEAPONS LAB SECURITY OFFICE – BAJA, MEXICO ......... 268

    BIOWEAPON LAB PERIMETER – BAJA, MEXICO ........................... 269

    CIA HEADQUARTERS - LANGLEY, VIRGINIA .................................. 271

    COVERT BIOWEAPONS LAB – BAJA, MEXICO ............................... 272

**CHAPTER 14 - NEVER PISS OFF A MAN OF VIOLENCE WITH A GUN** ...................................................................................**281**

    SURFSIDE ESTATE - CORONADO, CALIFORNIA .............................. 281

    SHAN STATE - MYANMAR ........................................................ 283

    GEORGETOWN - WASHINGTON DC ........................................... 292

    MIAMI, FLORIDA ................................................................... 295

    SAN CLEMENTE, CALIFORNIA .................................................. 299

    PALM BEACH, FLORIDA – THE PRESIDENT'S RESORT ..................... 299

**EPILOGUE** .......................................................................**306**

    PALM BEACH, FLORIDA – THE PRESIDENT'S RESORT ..................... 306

    CORONADO, CALIFORNIA ........................................................ 308

# TRIGGER WARNINGS

- Patriotism
- Excessive violence
- Heroism USA style
- Americanism
- Guns
- Bombs
- Explosions
- Tech gurus spanked
- Guts, guts, and more guts
- Old school smack talk
- Hot chicks
- Mean old bastards
- Mar Lago
- Macho madness
- Custom El Camino 4WD
- More guns
- Helicopters
- More excessive violence
- Missiles fired from orbit
- Terrorists shot

*And much, much more*

## Man of Violence

Imagine a businessman, a complete outsider, is President of the United States. The intelligence community is corrupted at the highest levels. Silicon Valley leadership is infiltrated by hostile foreign powers. Mankind is at the brink of extinction. There is only one person the President can trust. A man of violence… because when no other alternative remains, you can no longer play by the rules.

This is the 12th novel by Bronco Hammer. Find your helmet, firearm, and ballistic vest because even the readers might have to shoot their way out of this blood and guts action thriller.

### *What readers are saying:*

Bronco Hammer novels are so graphic that I shot the book while I was reading it out of sheer panic. - *Mike "Da Butcher" Cardis - Meat Guru*

Bronco Hammer books, so manly, you'd feel like they should require an FFL to purchase. - *Tim Fife - Professional he-man and gunslinger*

There's a word for the man who doesn't read Bronco Hammer novels. And the word isn't 'man'. - *Greg Atkins - Historic Australian mastermind*

After you read a Bronco Hammer book your girlfriend will thank him...so will your wife! PS: don't let my wife read this... *Dave Smith - Living legend*

Bronco Hammer novels should be required as the standard for teaching our children to read and boys and girls to grow up to be Bad Ass 'Mericans! - *Bob Hopper - Gun slinging human weapon*

A man is known by the company he keeps, so keep a paperback copy of "Bronco Hammer" in you back pocket always. - *Kenny Wilson - Wisdom dispenser and lawman*

Bronco Hammer novels are as hard hitting as getting smacked in the face with a steel lunchbox stolen from a 1980s construction site. - *Emery Calame - Texan*

So, you want to read a Bronco Hammer novel, Get clearance from your doctor, light up your favorite stogie pour two fingers of your drink of choice, get strapped into your favorite chair, grow some hair and a pair let the adventure begin, where bad guys die good guys win and your new life begins. I know I am an ex-young guy \who survived. Thanks Bronco. - *Roger Fenton - gunfighter and lawman (retired)*

Throw away those blue pills, just read a Bronco Hammer book for the most natural way to boost your testosterone and vitality. - *Paul Kennedy - Manly man*

Even tough nut Aussies cringe at this story line. - *Bunny Warren, Australian legend*

Makes Mike Hammer look like a wimp - *John Laird – Man of danger - Texan*

The mere thought of having to face Bronco Hammer Mano y Mano has made many a known pistolero squat to pee. - *Bill Richardson - Arizona lawman (retired)*

Be ready to buy more guns. This book guaranteed to boost gun sales. - *Mike Ratke - American, Texan, stable genius, knife fighting enthusiast*

Side effects of Bronco Hammer novels include increased vitality, muscle mass and appeal to hot broads - *Carl Miller - Texas patriot*

Bronco Hammer books...be warned that "enlightened men" attempting to read them will feel inferior the rest of their lives! The rest of you studs, enjoy! *Rick Fowler, veteran and retired police officer.*

Reading Bronco Hammer novels makes you grow hair & brass where you've never had it before! - *Dan Saban – Man of action*

Trees lay down and beg Bronco Hammer to use their wood for the paper to print these books! *Eric Noonan – Internationally recognized real man*

Bronco books are so intoxicating and powerful they will leave women wanting more... of you! - *Bolt Hammer Jenkins*

Gavin Newsom banned Bronco Hammer books in California! What else do you need to know? - *Miguel Carlos - Retired Cop, Veteran, and American*

"Please Keep track of the hours spent reading this series. They qualify for COE credit and must be turned into AZPOST" - *Justin Corvelo - lawman*

Bronco Hammer; Non-fiction? Don't bet your life on it. - *Jeff Trapp - Gunman at large and extremely dangerous individual*

After reading one of Bronco's novels, I went outside to the grill, cooked me up a huge ribeye, medium rare, because only communists cook them well done, slammed it down with a baked potato (no salads-only eco-terrorists eat salads), downed a bottle of Makers and fireman-carried the missus upstairs. Thanks, Bronco Hammer! - *Mitch "Cochiloco" O'Conn - Retired Cop and knuckle dragging brute*

Throw away those blue pills, just read a Bronco Hammer book for the most natural way to boost your testosterone and vitality. - *Paul Kennedy - American*

Bronco Hammer books are better known as the Training Manuals used by Chuck Norris - *Carne Asada Steve - Retired lawman and man of mystery*

If it wasn't for Bronco Hammer novels there wouldn't be any real men. - *Steve Godsil - retired lawman and defender of the righteous*

Do you have a man bun and wear skinny jeans while drinking a latte? Read a Bronco Hammer book and learn what it means to be a real man. After two chapters you will be shaving your head and drinking warm scotch with a human hair in it and thinking to yourself "why was I such an ignorant pussy all these years? Bring in the super models, bitches!" - *Randy Lewis – Retired lawman and Harley enthusiast*

If Elton John read Bronco's books, he would ravage the Dallas Cowboys Cheerleaders, switch to heavy metal guitar, and join the Marines. - *Raven Douglas - Guitar Riffologist and Texas legend*

Bronco Hammer life advice "Kick ass and take names EVERYDAY ".... I may have gotten this same advice from a certain Special Investigation Unit Lieutenant. - *Jeff Henderson - Immortal hero and Arizona lawman*

Read a Bronco Hammer book or go vote for Bernie - *Paul Reichard - Man of Arizona*

Dapper Guru prefers Bronco Hammer novels – *Robert Marshall – Veteran and sophisticate*

Neil Armstrong probably had a Bronco Hammer book, in his pocket, when he became the first man to walk on the moon. Audie Murphy read Bronco Hammer books too. - *John Sheffield – Paratrooper*

"There are few people in England, I suppose, who have more true enjoyment of Bronco Hammer novels than myself, or a better natural taste." ~ *Lady Catherine de Bourgh of Rosings Park (paraphrased by Bobby Gardner)*

From the beaches of Coronado Island to the Oklahoma Badlands, Bronco Hammer novels rule! Now excuse me while I take care of these supermodels, shampoo a herd of buffalo, and fire off a few thousand rounds. - *Randy Willard - Man among Men - Okie Patriot*

# PRE-READ BRIEFING

Welcome back to another action-packed epic adventure that is chock full of patriotism, action, guns, pointless violence, and fun. Find a chair and I'll start the briefing.

In this novel we will conduct an in-depth exploration into the world of technology and foreign intrigue. In other words, we are hunting enemy spies. We will conduct this semi-covert exploratory activity by blowing up quite a bit of stuff and by killing many, many dirtbags. As usual, I hope you have a gun, beverage, and a helmet in reach because the crap hits the fan in this one. 'Man of Violence' is so full of testosterone and extreme danger that even readers might have to shoot their way out of the story.

The term *'man of violence'* is a tribute to all you who wore the uniform of our country, pinned on a badge, or just lived your life out doing your job and being a classic American bad ass. *(Australian bad asses are included as well)* Love of country runs rampant throughout this story and unapologetically so.

The concept of a man of violence is explored from the perspective of the good guys and the bad guys. Bottom line – there are some people you just don't mess with.

I also promise you that the metric system will not be used in this story or any other story I write unless it is utilized as a literary device for cursing the metric system (other approved exceptions for ammunition identification purposes only). America.

Thank you for being a reader. I appreciate every customer. Remember to watch your front sight and to always carry a knife. Now strap on your helmets. **You are now cleared to begin reading**.

Your pal,

Bronco Hammer – *the most dangerous writer in the world.*

# Chapter 1 – Never piss off an old man with a gun

SEVEN MILE BEACH - OFFICE TOWER, GRAND CAYMAN

Soundlessly, he twisted the doorknob with his reactionary hand, gently nudging the door open.

Pausing to the side of the doorframe for an extended moment, he assessed any potential threats before attempting to penetrate the threshold. McCartney lost a pal or two over the years in the fatal funnel. He knew better. But they did too. *Careless gets you killed. Remember basics and you might see your first pension check someday.*

He frowned. He sensed an imminent threat. Nothing tangible, just a feeling. *The old bastard knows I'm out here… So much for stealth mode.*

From within the room a voice addressed him. It was not a cheerful voice, nor a pleasant voice, just a familiar one… deep, loud, and ice cold.

"Get your worthless carcass in here and sit down, asshole."

*Shit…* He proceeded inside knowing that he was now entering a mega-suck environment. He put his best face forward.

The old man behind the desk eyeballed McCartney as he entered. Mac was a hard-looking man, brutish and rough in appearance, despite the tailored Brooks Brothers suit and highly polished shoes.

An unlit cigarette dangled at the corner of his mouth as he entered the room. Flouting the laws of physics, the Lucky Strike clung precariously from his lips as he walked, appearing as though each step might jar the non-filtered smoke loose from his mouth and onto the floor.

It didn't.

He paused again, tugging a Zippo out of his front trouser pocket. He torched the tip of the cigarette before pulling back a chair with his meaty hand and taking a seat at the table.

Leaning back in his seat nonchalantly until the strain of his two-hundred and eighty pounds made the chair creak to the breaking point, he waited for the other man to speak. McCartney's overly relaxed half-slouching body language complimented the '*I don't give a shit*' attitude. *Let the old man do his worst*, he thought. *He can't kill me and eat me... probably.*

The two men silently sat across from each other at the conference table, neither saying a word through an uncomfortably quiet minute and a half of mutual stink-eye.

The older man, organized and professional, could easily pass as an investment banker adorned in his posh gray suit, professionally shined handmade Italian leather Enzo Bonafe` oxfords, and crisply starched shirt. The matching silk tie and pocket square completed the stylish image. The only incongruence in the older man's urbane style revealed itself in his face and hands. His skin, dark and weathered, would be more likely found on an Alaskan fisherman or a desert range cowboy. The nasty scars and somewhat deformed knuckles might seem more natural on a bare-knuckle prize-fighter. The drooping mustache was thick, long, gray, and menacing in its own way. The man's eyes though, they told a story of their own... a horror story. Unfeeling and ruthless as the black button eyes of a great white shark... an apex predator... a serial killer.

The old man's icy stare did not intimidate McCartney... at least not to the point McCartney would allow him to see. Taking a deep drag on his cigarette, Mac cocked his head to the side, and gradually let a thin cloud of tobacco smoke waft towards the air conditioning intake, assessing his situation as the ethereal swirl gradually drifted up to the vent.

Mac attempted to assess the old man's mood. *The boss doesn't look happy. But then again, the boss never looks happy.* The old man didn't blink. *Does he even have eyelids?*

*Unfortunately*, McCartney thought, *the boss appears exceedingly unhappy right now*. The world-weary white-haired old man to whom McCartney reported looked *super* pissed off…

Based on his observations, McCartney determined that this wasn't the appropriate moment to ask for a raise. Anger and generosity seldom exist concurrently, and there was no sense in getting killed over a few lousy bucks a month. McCartney resisted his usual impulse to blab out some smart-ass shit and elected to keep his mouth shut this time. He thought he might attempt a new strategy… wait for the boss to break the awkward stillness. It seemed appropriate.

It worked.

The old man finally spoke, the uncomfortable silence cracking like an egg rolling off a kitchen counter. His voice sounded as friendly as a rabid jackal with its nuts locked in a set of vice grips held firmly in the hand of a guy who didn't like jackals very much. Each pointed word came out cold and alone, like stomps on a neck. "It… was… supposed… to… look… like… an… accident."

McCartney wasn't sure if that was a question, so he didn't respond. Stoic silence seemed to be working so far… He decided to stick with that approach for a bit longer. He bought time with another subtle puff on the cigarette.

The boss waited another full thirty seconds before slamming his fist on the table and barking, "*An accident*, asshole. Do you even know what an *accident* is supposed to look like?"

McCartney went on defense. "Uhm... It looked to me like he accidently got shot in the face... right?" For a moment, he thought his creative answer might work. But it didn't. McCartney watched the boss's facial expression harden. *How was that even possible? How does granite harden?*

The old man growled in that vaguely southern or western accent of an angry drill instructor while air-jabbing an accusing finger in McCartney's general direction. "No... no bullshit this time, McCartney, you can't just *ignore* orders, mister!"

McCartney sustained his relaxed posture despite the seething tension in the room. He countered the old man's words, defending himself by employing his elite debating skills. "Look boss, just because I did something that was *not* what you told me to do, is no reason to accuse me of ignoring orders."

The old man's face reddened even more. "You just *defined* ignoring order*s* you insubordinate prick!"

Mac feigned offense. "Now that's just hurtful."

The boss didn't react, he just aimed a thousand-yard stare in McCartney's direction, the kind of stare that typically either precedes or follows the act of slashing another man's throat open with a machete.

McCartney tried again. "Look, boss, bottom line, the guy *is* dead. The cops think it was a robbery or some other street crap. It's all good. Win-Win. Everybody's happy. All's well that ends well." Mac exhausted his inventory of bullshit clichés. His voice trailed off as he punctuated his feeble defense with another slow drag on his smoke. Enjoying a final puff before execution seemed about right.

Maintaining his kill stare, the boss carefully removed a black file folder from his Brunello Cucinelli leather portfolio. He finally broke eye contact, flipping open the folder, and glancing down as he began reading excerpts from a police report.

"The subject was found dead by local authorities. It appears he was shot somewhere in the face with a large caliber round at point-blank range. He was identified by fingerprints as no facial or dental identification was possible. DNA confirmation pending."

The boss slowly looked up from the document and locked his icy gaze on McCartney. "What were you carrying on this mission?"

"Me?"

The older man leaned in again and shouted in McCartney's face. "What weapon?"

McCartney involuntarily squirmed a little in his chair, not much of a squirm; it was subtle, but he knew that the boss saw it. That pissed Mac off. He hated squirming in front of the boss. Now the old man knew he had him by the gonads. Shit... capitulation time.

"My regular concealed weapon." McCartney muttered vaguely.

Leaning back in his chair, the boss pressed him, "Indulge me... be more specific."

Another quick draw on the smoke... ashes fell off the end of the glowing embers onto the table. He quickly brushed them to the floor with an instinctive hand swipe. McCartney flicked the remaining ash off the cigarette into a black plastic ashtray on the table.

The old man recognized the stall tactic. He pressed. "No, wait... better yet... show me."

McCartney frowned, preferring not to do a show and tell, but there was no choice. He slowly reached under his jacket, removing a massive chunk of death metal, and placed it on the desk.

The old man said nothing.

The void in speech compelled Mac to involuntarily start talking again... "Uhhh," he stalled, attempting to think of something intelligent to say. He had nothing, but words bailed out of his mouth anyway. "My Ruger Super Redhawk Alaskan 454 Casull," McCartney replied cautiously. "You know... my EDC... My backup... Not my primary combat weapon." McCartney took a stab at mitigating his actions. "My primary weapon would be overkill. I wouldn't do that."

The old man displayed no visible reaction as he watched McCartney's face contort in a failed attempted at appearing forthcoming and cooperative.

McCartney wasn't very skilled at rhetoric, but he was familiar with the tactic of throwing out ridiculous bullshit to frame oneself as being on the same side as one's accuser.

Unfortunately, the boss knew that ploy too. He listened to Mac's words before spitting out a one-word assessment of
McCartney's blathering. "Bullshit."

McCartney didn't shrug. He didn't speak. He took another long drag on the Lucky and exhaled another swirling mist of smoke.

The boss was trying to sustain his pretense of rage but found it hard to stay angry at a guy who carries a snub-nosed revolver designed to kill rampaging grizzly bears at point-blank range. But the boss also recognized that he was the man responsible to the CEO of their company who also happened to be the President of the United States. Therefore, he had to maintain some level of discipline. He continued using his outrage face and grilled McCartney like a prosecutor ripping a lying weak-kneed witness a new asshole. Deliberate. Relentless. Unmerciful. He threw in a sneer of disgust for good measure.

"So, instead of making it look like an accident, you blew his fucking head off?"

McCartney sucked the last draw out of his cigarette, refusing to establish eye contact as he responded, "When you say it that way, it sounds bad."

"Did you?"

"Yes. But it seemed like an excellent idea when I did it. And, in all fairness, he definitely won't be giving the Chinese any more US technology."

The boss delivered an additional fifteen seconds of intensive '*you make me wanna puke*' face before finally deciding this matter was not really a big deal. Sometimes traitors get their heads blown off… it happens. And nobody is more loyal to the President than Mac McCartney. Like any experienced leader, the old man knew when it was time to switch from scolding to counseling.

"All right. Fine. We skated on this one… but your directive is to fix problems, not cause them. What do you think the President would say if he found out you used a big-assed honking handgun capable of dropping a charging fucking dinosaur in its tracks to blow a fucking traitor's head off?

McCartney meticulously ground out his cigarette butt in the ashtray as he spoke. "I think he would get a boner, sir."

The boss started to come out of his chair to slap McCartney across the mug for being an asshole, when he realized the big slob was probably correct. The President loved shit like that. He settled back in his seat. You can't be angry at honesty.

"Fine. But discretion is our primary mandate… So…" The boss struggled for the right admonition. He turned his scolding tone back on. "So, watch it, asshole. No more dramatic bullshit. You and I are theoretically a secret operation, not a damned wrecking crew. Operative word, *secret*. Do you think you can remember that, or do I need to come across this table and kick your ass?"

"Sorry boss, I get excited sometimes. I'll watch it from now on," McCartney lied. "No bullshit, sir." He intentionally added the word '*sir*' to sound more sincere.

The leathery faced old man leaned in, "Be sure that you do, McCartney, because POTUS has a new assignment in the works for us. And he says we must execute this operation in a *very* subtle way. That means no crazy stuff this time, Mac."

"You got it, boss. No crazy…" McCartney said as he retrieved his firearm and placed it back in the custom leather cross draw holster under his coat. Because of his bulk, he was able to wear the holster on his strong side rather than the across the body configuration, providing a gunfighter cant to the weapon while still allowing him to keep it concealed. A big man's advantage.

25

The old man's eyes could clearly see McCartney nodding in agreement to the '*no crazy*' terms of the job, but he knew in his heart that before McCartney would finish with this forthcoming assignment there would be dead assholes stacked in the streets, shit would be blown up, and all loose ends would be slowly strangled with piano wire. McCartney was just that way. A top-tier problem-solver who just doesn't give a shit about anything. *A real American. Just like me.*

The old man pulled a Cohiba from his coat pocket. "Give me a light, then get the hell out of here. I have work to do."

"Copy that." Mac reached across the table and lit the cigar with his Zippo, then got up to leave.

The old man put a hand up as he took a long puff, stopping McCartney's exit.

"Yes, sir?" Mac asked.

"I forgot to tell you. Nice work blowing that commie traitor's head off…. Now never let that shit happen again. You've been officially counseled."

Mac nodded. As he turned to leave, a slight smile crossed his face as he did a slight calculation in his head. *That's my fifteenth time getting a verbal warning for excessive force. That must be some kind of record. America!*

# Chapter 2 – Never piss off a President with a gun

PALM BEACH, FLORIDA - THREE DAYS LATER

The President of the United States took the meeting with the old man in a secure private room at his Florida estate. Outsiders rarely entered this area of his home. The Commander-in-Chief even denied the Secret Service access to the personal retreat on the fourth floor of his mansion. Almost a decade before he ran for public office, he had designed this compartmentalized section of the building to be the most secure personal quarters on earth.

The President enjoyed a diet cola while the old man sipped at what he thought might be the finest cup of coffee ever brewed.

"So, is he on the job?" The President inquired.

"Yes, sir. He's on his way to San Diego now to prepare and then to receive a more complete briefing upon my arrival… once you have brought me fully up to speed on this... situation. That is why I am here, right?"

The President ignored the question and strayed off topic a bit. "You know, I like the way he handled that last asshole. Blew his head clean off... Gave him the full Callahan. He has that killer instinct. A real killer. I like that. He's the absolute best out there, that, I can tell you and that's no bullshit. I think everyone would agree with me. I swear, I almost got a boner just hearing about it. He's a real tough customer." The President often spoke without a filter, and in his private quarters, his language reflected his construction background even more. But sometimes he blathered on tactically to buy time for sizing up people, catching their reaction, and reassessing his approach. The President was a bit of a blowhard on the surface, but underneath the public image was an analytical machine. He added, "You know I carry a little 38 Special in an ankle holster myself... I have good security but that doesn't mean I shouldn't be prepared."

The President eyed his personal security advisor as he spoke. The man was younger than the President by ten years, but looked ten years older, or if not older, then perhaps ten years harder. The energetic billionaire thought his guest could easily play the part of a steely-eyed frontier marshal in western movies, maybe it was the droopy mustache, the lean build, he couldn't put his finger on it, but the man was unquestionably a tough cookie. When he spoke, his manly voice sounded like the guy from the truck commercials.

As a former private sector CEO, the President often viewed people in terms of product branding or as commodities in a business deal. The President also believed that there were two kinds of people living on this old blue marble, killers and pussies... and this guy in front of him, Tom Pearson, was a killer. That's why the President hired him. He was a valuable commodity and was loyal to the organization's brand. He was also an exceptional patriot. Pearson served honorably as a Delta Force operator, retired from the Army, and then became a private military consultant/mercenary before joining the Commander in Chief's family business as a covert fixer for international business problems. He wasn't one of the public faces that the President kept around to handle the ridiculous bullshit that came up from time to time. Those lawyers and spokespersons were merely cannon fodder in the eternal battle to protect his wild and colorful billionaire lifestyle. But this man was a bird of a different feather. He was a *true* killer in every sense of the word. He was extremely dangerous. He was completely trustworthy. Most important of all, he was invisible.

The President cut Pearson out of the organizational staffing chart by so many shell companies and banks that it looked like he didn't even exist. Even the President's family, except for the oldest son and namesake and his oldest daughter, was not aware of Mister Pearson's existence let alone his close working relationship with the Commander-in-Chief.

Still, Mr. Pearson's position had to evolve. He was one of the most experienced in the field and perhaps at one time he was the best in the world, but he was not a kid anymore. He knew it and the President knew it. The President and Pearson both acknowledged that some might consider him a little long in the tooth to handle full-blown national security situations in the field now. But to that end, three years earlier Pearson recruited a younger man to assist with the more demanding field operation tasks, another special employee of the President's vast business empire, also totally off the books and unknown to the business, government, or intelligence community. The younger man was named Benito Connor McCartney, but he went by Mac. He was a hulking brute of Irish-Italian descent who hailed from Tampa, Florida. Now *that* guy is one scary mother, the President thought.

The President asked, "So, Tom, how tough is your back-up man… Can I count on him… if the worst happens?" It was an uncomfortable question to ask, but doing uncomfortable things was part of the job.

He looked Pearson in the eyes as he awaited the answer.

Pearson frowned. He didn't like to speak in sentences… he considered point-and-grunt, yes or no, and a slight nod in the affirmative or negative as an adequate vocabulary for most situations. But the President deserved a genuine answer. Pearson respected him and his service. It was good to have a *real* man in charge of the country again.

Pearson began. "He has a unique background, sir. After a stint in the Army, during which he saw extensive combat, McCartney went off the grid for a few years. He made a living in illegal fist-fighting competitions, illegal gun-fighting competitions, and *barely* legal strong-man competitions. On paper Mac was an independent truck driver during that period of his life, and he actually *did* operate a big rig that also served as his home, but he earned his real cash as a professional man of violence."

"What do you mean, *a man of violence*?" the President asked, speaking reverently when repeating the term.

Pearson waited for an uncomfortably long time before speaking, maintaining eye contact with the most powerful man in the world. "A man of violence…" he paused for an instant to consider what words he would use, then continued, "He understands the world on different terms than most people. A man

31

of violence knows the ugliness humanity is capable of, the propensity for horror, abuse, genocide, crime, hate… and he likes it there. He knows that is where he belongs. A man of violence can be evil… *or* he can be a force for good. But either way, he struggles with one thing. A nagging question… a mathematical problem really… but it compels him to find the answer to that question." Pearson calmly cocked his head to one side, waiting to see if the President wanted him to continue.

"What question is that, Tom?" the President asked in a grim whisper.

"How many."

"How many what?"

"How many assholes will take to kill him."

The President was not a pussy, but he felt a cold chill run down his spine at Pearson's words. There was something in Pearson's eyes, a coldness that the President hadn't seen before. "Are you a man of violence, Tom?"

"Not by the definition I just gave you, sir. I'm afraid I already know the answer to that question. The people who have lasted in our business as many years as I have… military, special operations cops, mercenaries, assassins, murderers, career criminals… after surviving all those years, we know."

"And the answer for you, Tom... how many men it will take to kill you?" the President asked guardedly, not sure he wanted to know the answer... not sure if anyone should ever hear the answer to such a question.

Pearson's face slowly lost any expression of humanity, that strange coldness returned, turning his face into the snarling maw of a rabid animal, "All of them, sir. Every last rat bastard they got."

Pearson didn't simply speak those words. He spat out them out with intensity and precision, syllable by syllable, as if he entered into an unstoppable downward spiral of barely contained rage that could only end in the commission of cold-blooded murder, a man on the edge, a man who has killed, yet keeps killing, a man still trying to fire an empty gun into a filthy maggot who is already dead, and yet is still pulling the trigger, unable to stop, his wrath barely contained... horror and hatred spewing from his blue eyes in a palpable yet controlled demonstration of vitriol... visual opprobrium... an awfulness that has no name... perhaps the words of a man who was clinically insane.

And then, it disappeared... Pearson appeared relaxed and attentive again as though he had only been discussing the day's weather.

In his mind the President thought, *holy fucking shit*... but he didn't let Pearson see his reaction. He resumed their conversation as though he heard something equally unnerving every day. His ability to conceal his emotions was a gift. *If I had gone into poker*, he thought, *I might have even been richer*... His lips tight, the President inhaled deeply through his nose before speaking again. "I see." The President said nonplussed yet believing in his heart every word he just heard was factual... frightening, but factual. He went on to the next matter. "So, about your back-up man. I'll consider the answer to *my* question a solid yes... he's ready." The President swiftly changed the subject. He felt like perhaps he pushed Pearson too hard. But pushing the envelope made him a multi-billionaire and President of the United States... still, he may not opt to explore the mind of Pearson again. It was too dark and ugly in there. No man should have to see that.

The President met Pearson's back up man Mac briefly once before... he recalled him as a husky six-five and a couple of fast food stops away from hitting three hundred pounds. Mac's bushy black beard and long black wavy hair made him resemble that actor in those 1960s comedy spaghetti westerns... The President couldn't remember the actor's name... Bub, or Buck, or Bud something... but he always liked that guy. He was another tough customer.

But now this new matter was as ugly as it gets, a situation that was perhaps too much for even the old man and the kid to take care of, something that spanned both the personal and professional concerns of the President. It might be hideous. But these were hard men, perhaps two of the hardest men alive, and ugly was their business. It didn't matter, really. They were his last hope.

The President laid out his plans. "Tom, for security reasons, this will be our last face-to-face briefing while I'm the President. From this meeting forward, I want your contact to be my son."

Pearson didn't react. The boss's kid was a like a clone of the President. No problem. Pearson didn't answer. He just responded with a quick nod.

"There is just too much attention on me now, which is good… I need to keep in front of the public eye. But there are some things I need to do to protect our country that outsiders just can't know, and there are very few insiders who I can trust. Most of them are assholes, Tom, pathetic assholes. They don't love the American people; they only love ambition. There has to be a balance."

"No explanation necessary, sir. I completely understand and agree."

The President continued, "Your most challenging task will probably be figuring out how to keep Junior from going with you and your man on field missions." The President grinned proudly, knowing that was a fact. His gun-toting outdoorsman son loved action and was a tough customer in his own right. "He's as smart as they come, a real stable genius. You can trust him."

"No problem, sir," Pearson stoically replied.

"It's time to close the Grand Cayman shop. We're moving our security operations to the Coronado house in California. That will be your new ops center. I'll need you to set up shop there and settle in for the next six years. Does that work for you? It's a very nice place. I think you will enjoy living there," the President said with a sly smile.

Pearson almost smiled. "That will be fine, sir." Coronado was a dream location. The last surviving conservative, pro-military, pro-police town on the southern California coastline since Newport Beach fell to the wealthy commies immigrating from LA.

"When we wrap up our public service and we don't need an operation center anymore, you can live there the rest of your life if you wish.
You certainly earned it. Or, I'll build you a place here at the club if you like Florida better."

The President waved his arm like he could make a home appear on the sprawling estate with just a snap of his finger. Pearson suspected that wasn't outside the realm of possibility with the President. The man was a tireless worker who had an uncanny ability to complete projects. "Thank you, sir. I appreciate your kindness. I'll always be there for you."

POTUS quickly shifted to the problem at hand. "Here's what I got… and it's big, huge, perhaps one of the biggest deals that has ever happened."

Pearson smiled. He loved the boss's enthusiasm and his gift of mild embellishment to get his listeners in the right mindset before he got to the point.

The President continued, "My intelligence community insiders, the ones I can trust, discovered a massive conspiracy. A group of technology industry giants, all assholes... *that,* I can tell you... they've decided to create a new world leadership model. They want to control everything, which in most cases, I would say that it was their right to try, but there is a rub to this. They are advancing artificial intelligence driven farming, manufacturing, and distribution technology, totally under the radar, and doing so with the intent to make most of the people of earth unnecessary. But they aren't planning to just give everyone a nice lifetime vacation. They look at a large population as a threat. They want to have all the benefits of modern life but with only those *few enlightened people* of their choosing allowed to live it... They will permit the workers necessary for maintaining their lifestyle to live, in minimally adequate conditions, of course. '*Workers necessary*'... sounds a little like slavery, doesn't it?" The President was amply using finger quotes to stress his point.

"Yes, sir... It sounds quite a bit like that." Pearson didn't like it.

"So… to that end, they are also active in underground bio-warfare research. They are almost ready to begin a process of slowly eliminating most of the earth's population via some bug. They will have the antidote, but only their chosen few will get it. Every other survivor, outside of their *intellectual class,* receiving the vaccination may exist only to support the technology to care for the elite and to service their perversions… Genocide on a world-wide scale… totalitarianism… global slavery… Arguably the biggest crime in the history of humanity."

"Sir, that sounds far-fetched." Tom Pearson was dubious. *No one could pull that off… Or could they?*

Like a mind reader, the President instantly picked up on Pearson's doubts, "I know. It sounded crazy to me too. That's why I dug deeper after they brought this to my attention. Here… watch this."

The President hit a button on a remote control and an eighty-inch television screen that was mounted on the wall flicked on. A video played. It was surprisingly clear surveillance camera footage. It looked as if perhaps a covert operative took it with a concealed briefcase camera. The video revealed a business meeting made up of people who were easily recognizable to anyone who follows the tech industry. The remarkably crisp and clear audio captured a discussion among twelve technology CEOs about orchestrating spree-shootings at various areas to proliferate gun bans, referring to it as *the civilian disarmament stage*. They also discussed the *selection phase* in which they would use their social media algorithms to capture data indicating who would be the most helpful as labor, who would be easiest to control as slaves, and who might be useful for breeding purposes. A map popped up next, exhibiting large land purchases on islands and in remote areas which provide a nice year around climate and a reliable fresh water supply.

Pearson frowned, *this evidence is overwhelming*, he thought... he also noted that the President obviously had a man on the inside. He remained silent as he continued watching. It was too early to comment.

Next, a captured screen from one of the computers on the video revealed the methodology of how the group was identifying and selecting tradesmen and technicians, people who could maintain the vast network of robots, autonomous vehicles, and computer systems across the planet. The program detailed how this group would receive the antidote. Eventually, the surviving workers would be selectively bred in perpetuity to provide human support and services to the new ruling intellectual class.

Finally, the presentation concluded with excerpts from a report summarizing the new world order, in which most people would be gone, and this select handful operating a world-wide paradise for the chosen ten-thousand or so elite survivors. About six-thousand other people and their progeny would live out their lives as slaves providing for the elite few.

Pearson didn't like it. "What a bunch of arrogant assholes." He wished he had a pack of chew so he could spit.

The President agreed, "I know, right?"

"So why don't you just have them arrested?"

"They own Congress, they own the media, they own the universities, and they own many of the federal judges. Do you have any idea how easy it is to manipulate those spineless worms? It works like this… Some random big-boobed starlet gets sent over to the courthouse by a Hollywood investor, boom… they now own a judge… they've already pulled this shit from local judges to the Supreme Court… Remember how they rolled John? Or, an FBI Director's stupid ass kid gets a free ride for a law degree, and then after a few years of partying at an Ivy League college, she's placed on the board at a big tech company even though the dipshit kid is functionally illiterate… boom… they own the FBI. Or how about a corrupt congressman's wife gets set up as CEO of some phony baloney consulting firm, boom… suddenly they are millionaires, many times over at taxpayer expense, and once again… we're owned. I haven't told you the worst part."

"It gets worse?"

"I'm afraid so… we think they are unwitting agents of a foreign power."

"China?"

"Who else?'

Pearson snarled, "Rat bastards."

"Exactly… the thing is, these clowns think they are the ones running the Chinese… and they call *me* arrogant."

"Sir, I'm not surprised. They are the biggest bunch of windbags and asshats I've ever known."

"Well, then make sure you don't head down to the Capitol Building. They got some competition there."

Pearson snorted.

The President cleared his throat before speaking again. "We," the President gestured emphatically back and forth between the two of them before elaborating, "You and me, we are all that the people of America have left that I absolutely know won't sell them out. And *I'm* writing the checks for your operations out of my personal funds to make that happen. It's unbelievable that it's come to this. Sad."

Tom Pearson locked eyes with the POTUS. "So, what would you like us to do, sir?"

The President leaned back in his chair. "Good question. What would *you* do in this situation, Tom?"

Pearson didn't hesitate in answering. "I'd kill them all, sir."

The President took a lengthy sip of his diet cola before answering, buying himself a few moments to weigh the pros and cons of Pearson's answer before responding. "Then let's go with that."

# Chapter 3 – Never piss off a rich kid with a gun

CORONADO, CALIFORNIA - THE
PRESIDENT'S SECRET ESTATE

There has been a fad of attaching romantic or clever names to homes in resort or beachside towns over the past few years. This house was no different. The secret estate on Coronado known as Surfside was a beautiful six-bedroom, nine-bath, multi-level home just off Ocean Boulevard.

The unusual post-modern design of the main building provided a view of the Pacific from almost every room. When the windows were open, the house was close enough to the beach to hear the surf crashing on the sand. As far as anyone in California knew, the home's absentee owner was a Saudi prince. A lot of the Coronado real estate was foreign owned.

Junior wheeled up in a new Ford truck, his identity concealed by a ball cap, big sunglasses, and the fact that no one ever expected to see him

43

there, so there was no risk of *celebrity recognition* in play.

McCartney, or Mac, as the senior heir to the family fortune preferred to call the big man, waited at the gate with the four highly trained Dobermans that patrolled the property.

The son of the President smiled widely, "Mac, nice to see you!"

"You too… long time no see, Deeter. How are things?" Mac used the nickname/codename they gave Junior that was a vague play on his initials.

"Pretty good. My dad's a billionaire and leader of the free world. Hard to have a bad day." Junior smiled. He enjoyed having a code name. It was cool. He also appreciated being wealthy, although his personality and interests leaned very blue collar American.

Mac laughed. "Well, I can't disagree. Welcome to Surfside."

Junior entered the steel security gate and carefully petted the dogs as they sniffed him onto the canine approved guest list. "I've never actually been to this house before. It looks great and *what* a location. My dad knows real estate like nobody ever before. Totally excellent. The very finest."

Mac smiled and thought, *chip off the old block.*

The two traversed the mansion to the second-floor kitchen. They grabbed coffees from the Van Der

Westen Speedster coffeemaker on the counter and joined the old man at the table.

"Nice to see you, kid," the old man smiled and stood up to shake hands.

"You too, sir. It's always an honor, Mister Pearson." Junior said respectfully. He knew two key facts about Pearson. He retired from Delta where he became known as the elite of the elite… and he *was* old. That combination meant he was not a man to trifle with. Special Forces operators at Pearson's level only got old if they were extremely dangerous and highly skilled individuals. Or to put it another way, he's hard to kill.

Conversely, Pearson liked the young heir to the President, but as was his nature, he preferred focusing on business rather than pleasantries. "What do you have for us today?"

Junior immediately got to business, focusing like a red laser in a dark room. "It appears as if we have eight key problems to solve. The rest of the conspirators will behave if we square away these clowns." He didn't elaborate on what he meant by *square away;* He pressed forward flipping open a tablet device and launched into a quick presentation.

The tablet reflected photos of eight significant people in the world-wide technology industry, including background information, details of their treasonous conspiracy, their last known locations and schedules for the next six months.

Mac still had trouble wrapping his mind around what they were doing. "So, I don't get this, Deeter. These tech guys think they can take over the world with no kind of army?"

"Not only do *they* think they can, Dad's top analysists believe it's highly possible that they can. Plus, they are trying to destroy the nation-state concept of world governments. We recognize that they are fully capable of pulling that off too. We'd all be back to feudal lords and Dark Ages nonsense led by renegade computer weasels… We can't have that. Throw in their bio-weapon threat and we are in a '*terminate with extreme prejudice*' zone, a finding that even those clowns from the UN and the World Court couldn't argue with if they were honest."

Deeter changed the screen to display a flowchart of the plan and then another chart showing the locations of the targets.

"Okay then, when do we start?" Mac asked.

The old man quickly surveyed the data and answered. "You and I develop a plan and execute it, Mac. We start in forty-eight hours. There is a tech conference in Los Angeles this weekend and two of our targets will be there."

Mac nodded in agreement, happy to have a project underway. "No problem."

Junior got up from the table. "I'll leave this situation in your capable hands then," he said as he handed the tablet to the old man and delegated the mission to the two most dangerous men he had ever met. He continued. "I'm on my way to Tokyo, gentlemen. It's time for a Kobe steak and some cold Asahi with my girl. Then we will come back and go hog hunting in Texas. A little work-vacation."

"Doesn't sound like work," Mac stated with a sly smile, admiring Deeter's taste in food, beverages, and women.

"We have a little message to deliver to the Prime Minister of Japan and some very confidential good news to share with the governor of Texas and Ted. You know, Ted's not a bad guy for a politician. Now that I have spent some time with him, I like him. He's a great senator. We'll be backing him for the rest of his political career. But I think our most important work is to focus on getting more business-oriented people in government," Junior elaborated.

The old man almost smiled. "Music to my ears."

Mac interjected, "But not these weirdo bay area tech-business people?"

Junior's usual amicable demeanor vanished into the hard stare of a man willing to fight for what he believes, "No, not traitors… We support Americans."

47

Mac agreed with the premise, "Copy that."


Their business finished, the President's son dutifully rinsed out his coffee cup and put it in the sink. Although he was quite skilled at it when he needed to be, he didn't enjoy small talk either. It was time to hit the road.

Mac walked outside to check the perimeter for Deeter's imminent departure. When Mac went out the door, Pearson asked for a word in private with the President's oldest son.

Deeter gave him his full attention. "What is it, Mr. Pearson?"

Pearson began cautiously trying to keep his deep gravelly voice low. "In case things go wrong, I think McCartney is ready to take the helm."

"Well, let's not let things go wrong," Deeter said, a little worried about the prospect of losing Pearson. He never heard him speak in these terms before and it was unsettling.

"I got a new operator in the works in case something happens. So, he'll still have a partner. Mac doesn't know it. I'm emailing you the file." Pearson fiddled with his phone, Deeter's phone made a short ding noise indicating the message had come through.

"I'll look at it, but we need you, Mr. Pearson."

"Just take care of Mac in case there's a problem. He's a total asshole and a worthless piece of shit but..."

Pearson fought the urge to say something good about his protege, a man he thought of as his own kid, a big, mean, insubordinate jackass of a kid, but still like one of his own.

Deeter smiled. "I get it. Consider it taken care of sir... and no matter what happens, thank you for your service to our country and to our family."

"The honor is mine, son. The honor has been all mine."


As Deeter drove off to the executive terminal, Mac and Pearson headed for the secure sub-basement armory via a concealed tunnel with access through a ground-level bedroom closet. Mac admired the clever engineering that somehow rolled the entire closet out of the wall with the placement of an authorized thumbprint on a concealed bio-scanner, creating a wide enough opening to perhaps drive a golf cart through.

Pearson lectured as they walked. "We both agree that guns are good for getting the job done. Be we are theoretically in the business of making these terminations look like accidents. So, by all means... take sufficient firepower, but let's remember to take along the assassination packets too, and this time, for a change, let's actually try to use them," Pearson warned.

"Are you still mad about that last one, boss? It's not good to hold on to those negative vibes."

Pearson frowned more than usual at the negative vibes comment. "Whatever you say, Eightball," He answered sarcastically using a vague reference from a war movie made almost twenty years before Mac was born, "but we need to do this first one right."

"Copy that."

The weapons room was as artistic and elegant in its design as many of the President's other properties. Exquisite glass cabinets full of guns, ammo, knifes, swords, rockets, bombs, and technical equipment lined the walls. Mac admired the beautiful hardwood cabinets secured with a gold-plated steel mesh. Everything was accessible through advanced biometric recognition systems. There was also a twelve-foot work bench with comfortable looking antique stools with dark tanned leather upholstery.

Pearson almost smiled. "The boss has the top of the line equipment for us." He admired the mounts on the wall above the bench, each weapon and tool placed in a specific space as marked by white outlines.

"Do you think he has an atomic bomb down here?" Mac said jokingly.

The old man turned and looked at him coldly. He didn't speak. Mac wasn't even sure the old fart was still breathing. For some time, he had suspected Pearson could breathe through his eyelids. The message was clear though… some words are not to be spoken.

McCartney didn't push it. He wisely changed the subject to the first set of targets. "I think we should frame these two clowns in a compromising position. Maybe do a drug overdose routine. What do you think?"

"Sounds reasonable. I'll start figuring out the logistics for a bathtub slip or perhaps I'll use the heart failure drug again. That's always a good one."

"I'll be honest with you. I love the *failed robbery* scenarios more than anything, but…" He tried to appear sincere as he continued. "I'm going to go with the program this time and stay low key. I'm a team player, boss." Mac's forced facial expressions of sincerity didn't effectively mask his blatant lie.

Pearson wasn't buying it, "Bullshit. First chance you get you will blow some asshole away. I know you, boy."

Mac tried to appear even more sincere. "No boss, I promise. I won't blow away anybody unless it seems like a good idea, or some other reason."

This was too much talking for Pearson, "Right. Just try to stay with the script, okay? We have a lot of tech gurus to whack."

"Exactly," Mac said, still maintaining the *team player* ruse.

Mac picked out some new firepower, just in case. He took a pound of C-4, an AR in.300 Blackout with a ten-inch barrel and a suppressor, and a Sig 220. He would certainly take his Ruger with him in case things got ugly, but not his primary weapon. No sense drawing attention to himself... and it was unwise to push the old man *too far*.

He searched through the assassination cabinet. He took the heart attack, drug overdose, and mental breakdown packets, fun little toys each about the size of a pocket first aid kit. He grabbed a few incapacitation packets as well, little soft plastic facemasks attached to tiny metal cylinders that looked like $CO_2$ cartridges for a pellet rifle.

He also found a standard CIA communication kit, the newest Kevlar Hawaiian shirt, and a helmet.

The old man noticed his attire. "What the hell do you need a helmet for on a covert operation?"

"Because... America, boss. Just... America."

Weary of having to carry a ridiculous amount of shit for decades through some of the most hostile and harsh environments on earth, the old man was a bit of a minimalist on the equipment side. But when the kid is right, he's right.

"I get it…" The old man seldom conceded a point to the kid but… there are exceptions to everything. He stopped short of saying he was sorry for mentioning it. *Apologizing was reserved for… well, who knows, it has never happened yet*, he thought.

Mac tried his hand at being conversant. "Not carrying much on this one, Mister Pearson?"

The old man focused on what he was doing rather than making eye contact to answer, "No, A Glock 26, my comm gear, and a couple of assassination packets. Also, a couple of candy bars. Sometimes I like a snack."

"Why don't you bring more equipment?"

"Because I'm not a raging pussy."

"I *get* it… sorry."

Mac didn't have a moratorium on apologizing. He didn't mean it anyway.

They each placed their gear in a generic black nylon bag and exited the armory, securely locking the vault-like door behind them.

"Who's driving?" Mac asked.

"I am, idiot. I enjoy living."

"Fine."

They wandered out to the garage, threw their gear in the trunk of a twelve-cylinder Mercedes sedan, and hopped in.

The old man got behind the wheel. "Time to go to LA, boy, and visit our new friends." Pearson pushed the start button, the garage door button, and the driveway gate button.

McCartney offered a random tidbit as they hit the street. "Have I mentioned that I've never been to the big Mouse Park?"

"That's in Anaheim, dipshit. It's not even close to LA, and no, we aren't going there."

"Just saying," Mac replied wistfully.

Pearson didn't give a shit about wistfulness. "Shut up."

"Got it."

Mac closed his eyes and dozed off to enjoy pleasant dreams about killing enemy computer dudes. Good times.

# Chapter 4 – Never piss off a commie with a gun

## THE GREAT HALL OF THE PEOPLE – BEIJING, CHINA

Although the dull gray block walls were adorned with garish red and blue faux accoutrements across the exterior, the Communist Party headquarters' interior was elegant and perhaps even what a socialist might describe as… decadent. The opulence within the structure mirrored the style of the magnificent buildings designed by the current US President around the world before he went into politics. For the comfort of the revered party leaders, the communists spared no expense. Leading the party requires comfort and elegance, allowing the commissars to focus absolute attention on the appropriate redistribution of the people's earnings.

Zhao, the Director of the Department of Economic Counterintelligence and Western

Disruption, sat at the head of the table. His importance to the financial future of China was significant. Zhao's creative leadership led to the draining the resources and wealth of the west via institutionalized theft, bribes, and intimidation, so China could thrive economically and militarily at the expense of the United States taxpayer. He smiled at the thought of the feckless American people squealing if they ever realized that their routine payroll deductions were financing the weapons that would eventually kill them all.

A lean man, taller than average and prematurely bald, his face was a visage reflecting an aura of wicked intent. His eyes were not unlike those of a predatory bird, sharp and focused. His threatening image was betrayed by his awkward and uncoordinated movement. He forced himself to barely move his arms or upper body as he walked in short deliberate steps everywhere he went.

"What of the social media initiative?" Zhao asked in his raspy high-pitched voice.

A bureaucrat named Wu answered proudly, "Our agent is in almost complete control of the FacePlace company. She has total influence on the American puppet we placed in charge when we stole the software from the original developers and put that pasty weakling in place as CEO. We are close to having complete dossiers on the personal habits, associations, and finances of nearly everyone in the free world. Based on that intelligence our list of targets for corruption and treason is so large that we can control two-thirds of the planet with simple blackmail... and most of it done remotely. As the true power behind the throne, so to speak, she is our most productive agent. That she is willing to live with that spineless bourgeoise worm to accomplish her mission is a testament to her loyalty."

This news brought a frosty smile to Zhao's face. "Excellent. Well done, Wu." He turned his attention to another lackey. "And the propaganda device, Comrade Chen?"

A devious looking man seated a few chairs down and to the left carefully placed the cup of tea he was sipping on the table before him, quickly touched his lips with a napkin before replying, "The success of the Twister program is beyond our wildest imagination. We can influence politics, finance, and public opinion world-wide now... not just influence, but almost total control. We had to teach the Twister CEO a lesson, he thought he was in control and tried to assert his will on us, but after public humiliation and a costly divorce, he now understands he must comply with his masters."

"Excellent. How about professional sports?"

A muscular man of about thirty years of age stood, "We own the capitalists' so-called football clubs and basketball clubs. Our operatives have managed to leverage their popularity to swing the impressionable fans to a more compliant thought process regarding our goals. The basketball coaches who have been our best operatives have been extraordinarily successful in building a following. Also, they have consistently thrown all the games as directed so we have been able to consistently make about fifty million US dollars per year on our online gambling initiatives without drawing unnecessary attention to the scheme."

"Well done, comrade. Well done, indeed. Now… What about Wall Street and the banks?" Zhao asked.

A man slightly older than the others in the group seated opposite of Zhao stood and responded cautiously as an accountant, "We enjoy total control of the institutional software and key leaders. We used the yankee scum's own greed against them to significant effect. Total victory."

Zhao smiled. "Perfect. Technology?"

A younger man seated to Zhao's right smiled wickedly as he answered. He passed a folder to their leader as he spoke, "We are using their own investment community money to develop our space program using their private sector space research and development in rocketry. We also have them wasting billions on electric vehicles, cars, and solar products, although they do not yet have the technology to make these whimsical inventions competitive with the internal combustion engine. As it turns out, fossil fuels are more efficient, transportable, and when used with innovative engineering, significantly less harmful to the environment than the batteries currently being used in their latest electric based technology."

There was a chuckle around the table as the group enjoyed the success of their manipulation of the west's easily manipulated environmentalist groups. The useful idiots almost single-handedly destroyed the US economy with their *feel-good* activism. It was almost too easy. After the old Soviet Union spent years flipping the American public-school systems into indoctrination centers, China was reaping the benefits of controlling the younger generation's thinking. And all while the poor Soviets were still covertly operating in the shadows, unable to even publicly claim Mother Russia as their own.

The speaker continued, "When they do overcome the energy storage and time-to-recharge problems, we will immediately receive the plans and begin production of a less expensive version. In the meantime, our slaves are producing tech products at a historic rate driving down prices and destroying the western manufacturing base… unless their President interferes," he added with a degree of concern revealed in his voice and mannerisms.

Zhao was happy with the report until the upstart mentioned the US Chief Executive.

*Was that an attempt to embarrass me*, Zhou thought? He delivered his next words carefully. "*We* will deal with the political matters. The Party has firm control of most of the western government officials." He paused for an uncomfortably long time before continuing. "It is not something you should concern yourself with, comrade," he stated icily.

The younger man lowered his head in shame. "My apologies, Comrade Director."

Zhao made a mental note to have the man and his family executed later and their organs sold. "Do not worry, comrade" he lied. "You are making exceptionally substantial progress with your assignments. Your work will be a fine example to all."

Now weary of hearing the reports and eager to place the death order on the ambitious upstart, Zhao ended the meeting and returned to his luxury estate. He had new companions awaiting him selected from some of the finest women taken from the rural villages in the past few months. It would be a good afternoon.

The greater plan would soon be revealed, and the tactical virus designed to eradicate an entire race would become a reality, or more specifically, to eradicate all but one race.

## DOWNTOWN LOS ANGELES

Pearson and Mac walked through the lobby of the Westin Bonaventure Hotel. Pearson, a man of extensive counter-intelligence experience, immediately noticed an overweight bartender chatting away with a dangerous looking guy seated at the bar. The man didn't seem to be a threat to them, but he was clearly a professional. A big man, maybe six-five, dress hat, white shirt, skinny black tie, and a black suit tailored to conceal a large handgun, perhaps a 1911. His black leather shoes glistened, polished to the luster of a Wall Street banker's. Pearson saw the man surreptitiously glance in their direction as he did a subtle hand gesture, palm down moving side to side. He had made Mac and Pearson as professionals as well. He was dangerous, no doubt about it, but he was unilaterally extending a professional courtesy, he was letting them know he was there for a reason, but it didn't involve Pearson or Mac.

Pearson gently touched the elbow of a passing waitress. He handed her a fifty. "Get that guy a drink and keep the change."

The woman scampered off, highly motivated by the tip.

"What was that about?" Mac asked.

"I don't think we're the only ones kicking ass for America here in downtown LA today. I'm just making sure we don't accidently cross each other's path," Pearson whispered.

"Good point. I know of that guy."

"Who is he?"

"John Carver Christianson. They call him JC. He's a private detective."

"What's the story on him?"

"JC the PI? Not much… He's nobody to fuck with… Former Marine, maybe crazy… But you know… he's *fine* unless you piss him off."

"Then what?" Pearson asked.

"Then, he'll kill you."

"Oh," Pearson replied, suddenly deciding he liked this guy.

Mac elaborated, "I've never met him. There was a briefing workup done on him a couple of years ago, surveillance photos, background... Something about a fiasco with a pack of psychotic international criminals… who eventually perished."

Pearson released the hint of a smile, "Perished. I like that word. It seems nicer than crude words like *murdered* or *killed*."

"Then there was also Eagle Rock."

"Shit. That was him? Was that even real?"

"It can't possibly be what they say it was... But who knows? Sorry I mentioned it."

"You should be… you could get a lethal finding put out on you for saying it, and on me for just hearing it. If you ever mention it again, I will put your ass down myself."

Both men cast glances from the corners of their eyes, hoping they wouldn't see imminent death creeping up on them for their recklessness in discussing the forbidden topic.

They silently walked to the front desk and got checked in. They each found the operational packets waiting for them in their rooms. For the next two hours, they chilled out while reading the packets.

The duo met for dinner at the brewery on the fourth floor near the pool and enjoyed an alfresco meal of traditional American bar fare as they sat as far away as possible from the rest of the patrons.

Pearson started, "So, it looks like these two are key speakers at the event. It might be tough to hit them there with all the security that will be working the venue. But they *are staying* at the Intercontinental on Wilshire. They each have penthouse suites booked."

Mac asked, "What are they speaking about?"

Pearson gave him a *what do you give a shit what they are speaking about look* before answering, "Artificial intelligence and sex robots."

For the first time this week, Pearson now had Mac's full and undivided attention.

"Can we listen to the speech before we kill them?

Pearson wasn't having it. He spoke a little more forcefully than necessary, "Our aim is to make it look like an accident and get the hell out of here, not to listen to speeches made by a couple of tech knobs."

Mac wouldn't let go of the idea, "Sure, sure, sure... but, uhhh... aren't you curious? I mean... sex robots... how cool is that?"

Pearson picked up his double burger with pepper jack cheese and pickles, "No... I'm not curious... I'm heterosexual." He took a big sloppy bite out of the burger and then wiped his face with a napkin as he chewed.

Mac continued. "You don't *have to* be gay to have a sex robot."

Pearson swallowed his food before responding, "No... I am quite sure that you do. Besides, how do you know so much about this shit?"

Mac tactically disregarded Pearson's question and asked another unrelated question, "Well, do you think they'll have free samples?"

"Of what?" Now, Pearson was considering kicking Mac's ass for being a relentless dick.

"I don't know... atomic hooters."

Pearson paused for a moment as he imagined what atomic hooters might be, then, he continued, "Look, we need a solid plan to get these two assholes. Just a basic accident probably won't work, so I'm leaning towards staging a *weird sexual liaison gone bad scenario*, and it seems like your perverted little mind is in that zone already, so…"

"I like it. Tell me more!" Mac said as he lit a cigarette in the dining area, violating hundreds of California statutes with impunity. "Will there be a sex robot involved?"

Pearson ignored the sex robot obsession and elaborated on his plan. "We just get them naked in one room and make it look like they killed each other. The press will fill in the rest."

Mac knew what the answers to his next set of questions would be, but he asked anyway, "I brought the assassination kit for that. Did you bring the appropriate kit?"

"I did," Pearson said confidently.

Mac was confused. "I didn't see you take it when we were in the armory."

"I didn't want you to see me take it." Pearson countered.

"Knives?"

"Of course."

"Knock-out gas?"

"DARPA special supply, untraceable."

"Perfect."

Pearson shared the plan. "You bag your guy in the elevator and I'll get mine in his room. I'll use the room service gag and then gas him inside. Then we pants them, make it look like they stabbed the shit out of each other, plant a bunch of weird porn and sex toys in the room, and then we go for late cocktails."

"Where do we get the weird porn and sex toys?"

"Where are we?"

"Downtown Los Angeles… oh, yeah." A flash of '*duh*' crossed Mac's face as he realized they could probably find anything imaginable in downtown LA. He switched gears back to the cocktails part of the plan. "Drinks at the lounge on the 71$^{st}$floor afterwards?"

"Exactly. The boss said to keep our per diem down to around five thousand a day each."

"Good times." Mac grinned.

"No shit. I remember having to fake a receipt from Burger King just to pay my rent when I was a government operator. I like this better."

"Yeah, me too."

\*\*\*

At nine o'clock the next evening, Bartholomew Jerome Winger, CEO of EdgeBuzz Automotive, manufacturer of what he called intuitive electric autonomous transportation devices, headed back to his room following his speech and after securing close to a billion in venture capital for his latest entrepreneurial enterprise, a new sex robot company. It was a very productive night. He would have to pay himself a few hundred million out of that money for his important contribution to the business, naturally. He stepped into the penthouse elevator where he noticed an exceptionally large bearded man in a dark blue suit standing there staring up at the floor numbers. The man looked a bit menacing, but security was superb at this hotel and the man *did wear* an expensive Rolex, so he probably wasn't a mugger. Still, he didn't look like he belonged on the penthouse floor either. He wasn't like everyone else. He had an aura of violence about him, something… dark. But, Winger thought, it might be discriminatory to suggest that someone was violent based on their appearance, and the man could be a minority, although he looked like a big scary Italian truck driver. So, Winger, the ever-vigilant social justice warrior, let his guard down, forced himself to ignore the man, and focused his attention on his mobile phone. Winger hated uncomfortable situations.

The door closed and the elevator car started rising through the central core of the building as it bypassed all floors and flew up to the penthouse level at an almost unnerving speed.

Having already placed a sticky note over the security camera lens, Mac grabbed the man by his bald head and pushed a specially designed plastic device attached to a small canister over the struggling Winger's nose and mouth. Within two seconds, the man was unconscious. Mac dragged him by the collar to his co-speaker's room. He did a quick knock… shave and a haircut. The door came open an inch as Pearson eyed the hallway and then admitted the big man with the unconscious tech guru into the room.

"Looks like that went seamlessly," Pearson commented.

Mac grunted, "Yeah, walk in the park." Mac saw the other guru, Granley Shumway, already flopped on the floor unconscious.

"Let's get on with it."

They went about the work of murder. An hour later, they had the scene set perfectly. Two tech giants appeared to be engaged in an unusual sex act that got out of control.

The two operatives left the door slightly ajar as they left. Pearson made an anonymous phone call to an LA paparazzi who was notorious for covering the antics of celebrities who stayed at the hotel.

An hour later, a news flash appeared on every TV set in the world.

"Two Technology Giants Killed During Bizarre Sexual Tryst in Los Angeles Hotel"

Relaxing at a table on the seventy-first floor of the Westin Bonaventure, Mac and Pearson enjoyed craft Manhattans made with WhistlePig fifteen-year-old straight rye. Delicious.

## THE GREAT HALL OF THE PEOPLE — BEIJING, CHINA

Zhao was furious. Two of their top useful idiots were dead. The group advisors gathered before him in the crowded situation room within the Communist Party Headquarters sat humbly, attempting at all costs to avoid eye contact with their mercurial leader.

He addressed the group confidently, "We own the Mayor of Los Angeles, known locally there as Mayor Yoga Pants, however, I'm uncertain why they call him that. Perhaps he is good at yoga," Zhao did not understand that the nickname, *Mayor Yoga Pants,* was a sarcastic slur popularized by two popular AM radio drive-time LA shock jocks. Zhao's lack of knowledge about the use of American idioms caused him embarrassment from time to time, but his arrogance drove him to attempt to incorporate American slang into his speech anyway.

He continued with his remarks, "When this incident came to the attention of his government, he reported to me immediately, in compliance with his standing orders. He informed me that the two dead men were involved in a perverse sexual activity that somehow erupted into an extremely violent confrontation. Somehow, their so-called free press discovered the bodies before the police could arrive and a reporter contaminated the scene. This is all information the Mayor garnered from his LAPD, an organization we have almost no control over beyond a few assets we have positioned at the very top levels... for now." He paused and eyed his cowering subordinates suspiciously, "The local authorities seem to be satisfied with these findings. I am not. Our covert operatives from the consul believe the deaths were homicides staged by unknown third parties. They base this on their ongoing surveillance and management of the two. Both were closet homosexuals, both routinely engaged in perverse sexual acts independently, but neither was violent, and neither was aware of the other's sexual proclivities. In fact, they are what the Americans call, a couple of pussies... which is a terrible insult in their country," he explained, impressing the others with his mastery of American slang. "This means it is highly likely that someone is targeting our US assets in technology and we no longer have a President in place to support our espionage efforts. So, we must stop this encroachment by their authorities immediately."

He waited again for an uncomfortable few moments before continuing. "So, here is what you will do," he said threateningly. "I want you to initiate full security protection protocols on the remaining high-level assets we have in the US technology community. I want our top protective agents... and not just some of them. I want *all of* them." He slammed his fist on the table at the word *all*, startling the rest of the men in the room.

"Without unencumbered access to all US technology, we are doomed financially and militarily. If you want to live, you will make sure that these murders expand no further."

Minister Lao raised his hand and spoke, "Are we not concerned that using so many of our paramilitary forces will draw unwanted attention to our mission... and what about the other ongoing operations against the west?"

Zhao stood silent for a moment as if he were carefully considering Lao's words. Then he snatched a nine-millimeter Chinese QSZ-92 pistol from his belt and shot Lao in the face. Lao flopped back into his chair as blood spurted across the table. He twitched for a few seconds then slumped out of the chair onto the floor. The men sitting near him restrained themselves from reacting to the blood spray covering their faces lest they become the next target of Zhao's rage.

Zhao pushed his own chair away and walked over to the body. He emptied the rest of the pistol's magazine into Lao, a sneer of disgust and revulsion on his face as he methodically shot most of his former advisor's head off. Zhao was not a huge fan of people questioning his orders.

On firing the last round, he turned his attention back to the group. "Any other comments... or questions?"

There were no other comments. There were no questions either.

Zhao snarled. "Then go... deploy all forces immediately."

The group scrambled out of the room like first graders hearing the morning recess bell, glad to escape Zhao's presence, and determined to carry out his orders at all costs.

Zhao smiled. The West, after being bled for all her wealth and innovation, would soon disappear forever. Project Mao would soon be initiated.

## HAWAII – FEATHERSTON ESTATE ON THE BIG ISLAND

"Why are all of these people here? I don't like this!" Devin Featherston, CEO of FacePlace, whined as he watched over fifty heavily armed Chinese agents milling about.

His wife chastised him openly in front of the small army of security operatives who were in his living room patiently awaiting their assignments, "It doesn't matter who they are, and it doesn't matter what you like. You just need to sit quietly in your room until I call for you."

"Okay…" he whimpered.

Dejectedly, he did as he was told and went to his room.

As soon as he disappeared into the depths of the gigantic mansion nestled along the shoreline of the vast tropical estate, she began giving orders, after all, she was a Shang Xiao, the equivalent of an American Army Colonel, in the Chinese People's Liberation Army.

After decades of serving in a deep-cover assignment, she had reached the pinnacle of achievement, capturing the most widespread intelligence collection software tool in the world, a social media program that people unwittingly populate with personal and professional information. Do you need access into a secret government research lab? Oh look, here is the head night janitor. He has a grandchild to kidnap… or a gambling problem… or other blackmail opportunities. It's like these western fools spy on themselves.

The work had been distasteful to say the least. She had to assume the role of love interest and then spouse of arguably the most unlikeable and least manly man who ever lived. In the vernacular of her target country, he was a total wimp. Fortunately, the gullible oaf was easy to manage, and she achieved full control over the software program.

Now she deployed troops over the thousand-acre estate grounds.

She leaned over a map on the kitchen table and conversed with the leader of the special operations branch assigned to protect Featherston, "I want a minefield here, and snipers placed tactically along these three ridgelines." She pointed to key tactical positions on the map. Add as many as you wish should you feel it is necessary. More troops can respond if we need them."

"Understood. We have sufficient personnel to provide protection, but I think we need some type of coastal defense weapon in place here and here." He pointed on the map to two small spits of sand that projected out into the Pacific."

"We have three *Boyevaya Mashina Fourteens* hidden in a warehouse in shipping crates on the island. I can have them in place in the morning, but I suggest you camouflage them."

"Certainly, comrade Colonel. We can make those work."

The two exchanged salutes and went about preparing for the possibility of armed attack.

## SURFSIDE - CORONADO, CALIFORNIA

Sitting on the deck of the mansion watching a sunset, Pearson and Mac sipped cocktails and listened to a music stream of their favorite entertainer, the Margaritaville man. Even though both men were remarkably different, as 'guys' they found it easy to slip into an island lifestyle.

"So, who is our next target?" Mac asked.

Pearson didn't answer right away. He was hoping to see the green flash… there wasn't one. But there is always another sunset provided for another attempt every twenty-four hours, so it was all good. As he listened to some words about a saltshaker and tattoo, Pearson took a long drink from the cheesy plastic coconut cup he purchased at a tourist shop on Orange Avenue. Finally, he answered the question. "It's some turd in Hawaii. I'm thinking this one will be easy."

# Chapter 5 – Never piss off a spy with a gun

## THE TOWER RESORT HOTEL - HAWAII

Pearson wasn't happy as he reviewed the intelligence packet. "So, how do we pull this off? The guy seldom leaves his computer room, he reportedly pukes if he is exposed to the out of doors, and he only eats those stupid frozen hot bag things…" He threw the thick file down on the table in disgust.

"Pockets," Mac corrected him.

Pearson didn't have time for it. "Whatever. Are they in bags and are they hot?"

"Yeah."

"Then they're hot bags… dipshit… But the point is, we can't get to him unless we breach the house security and find the room that he's in. That joint has fifteen bedrooms, eighteen bathrooms, and four kitchens… and he is in the basement most of the time playing on his computer."

"Maybe it won't be as easy as we thought." Mac said as he walked over and checked the mini bar at their hotel.

Pearson pitched another idea. "Maybe the mysterious intruders thing? Killed in an attempted burglary?"

"We might not have a choice. He is dug in there like an inflamed hemorrhoid."

"Could get messy…" Pearson warned. *But most of our missions usually ended up getting messy,* he thought. *It just seemed to work out that way. It's the nature of the business.*

Mac pressed the subject. "Yeah. I don't like it. You keep telling me that these gigs are supposed to look like accidents."

Pearson snapped his finger. "Hey, I know. Domestic dispute. He has a wife. Maybe we stage a fight that gets out of control. Frame her or something like that."

Mac did his homework on the target too and was familiar with his personality profile. "He's too big of a puss to get in a fight. Nobody would buy it." The more Mac researched the target, the less he liked him. He seemed to be a total worm and control freak… almost like one of those Portland commies.

Pearson shrugged. "Then I guess it's going to be *intruders* then."

"Yep, afraid so," Mac concurred.

"Well, let's gun up and get it done. It probably won't be that hard."

"I don't see how it could be."


Nightfall came, and it was time to make their move. Pearson and Mac silently walked through the jungle, having parked their rented jeep on a remote dirt road outside the walls surrounding the massive estate.

"I thought this joker was against having walls," Mac stated as he tried to figure out how they would scale the twelve-foot block fortification that marked the perimeter of the property. *There has to be a worthless hypocrite worm behind this shit*, he thought to himself, liking the target even less.

"He's a puss," Pearson responded, assuming he fully answered the question about the target being against walls with that generic detail.

"Exactly."

Pearson touched Mac's shoulder in the darkness and whispered, "Two hundred yards up is a service gate. There shouldn't be any security there at this time of night."

"Copy that."

They made their approach as quietly as possible. Switching to hand signals, Pearson directed Mac to scout the gate. He assumed a cover position.

Mac disappeared into the darkness only to return ten minutes later with unwelcome news. He led Pearson to a safe distance into the surrounding wilderness before speaking.

"We have a problem," Mac whispered.

"What?"

"There are ten operators securing that gate. They're speaking Chinese. And they don't seem nice."

"Operators or security?"

"Total operators and armed to the teeth... and I think they have snipers. I couldn't confirm it, but it appears as though there is a guy in a treetop about one hundred yards inside the fence. There could be more."

"Did you bring your primary weapon?" Pearson asked.

Mac frowned, "No, you've been sort of a dick about it recently and this is supposed to look like an accident, or burglary or something that doesn't involve shit blowing up. At least that's what you are always telling me."

"I know but that was before we got burned."

"You think somebody ratted us out?" Mac asked.

"Maybe. Or maybe they just figured it out on their own. Doesn't matter, things change."

Mac offered another valuable McCartney insight. "I heard these Chinese guys are inscrutable."

"Do you even know what that means?" The old man wasn't politically correct by any means, but he wondered if the kid had been watching old Charlie Chan movies or something.

"No... But it sounds like smart or something."

The old man gave him a *you're just too stupid to live* look. "Just shut up and let me think."

Mac suggested, "Let's get more guns and come back tomorrow."

The old man gave it some thought and decided the kid was right for once. It was past the time to get serious about killing these fucktards... and if China was operationally involved, it could have some serious implications.

## WASHINGTON, DC

The FBI Director was nervous. If the government of China decided to expose him, it would be his ass... and the Chinese would totally do it too. The commie assholes were evil bastards... but they paid well. At their direction, he had been screaming at whoever would listen about Russian collusion at the top of his lungs for years, hoping to keep the public focus off the nation that had been supplementing his government paycheck for thirty years. But now that wasn't enough. The Chinese wanted to know which agency was whacking technology gurus. They owned their fair share of them. Of course, it was in his interest to know as well. If he *was* outed as a foreign spy, he had no doubt the present Commander-in-Chief would order him executed, and it would be completely legal too. But would the commies burn him? They spent decades putting key players in place all over the intelligence community. Why throw out that investment? They couldn't be that ruthless, could they?

He pulled the untraceable cell phone the Chinese gave him from his pocket and made a call to his colleague, and fellow PRC double agent, the Director of the CIA.

"This is Director Clammer," he timidly said as though he was unsure if that was correct.

The FBI Director spoke informally to his partner in crime. "Clam Man, can you get a team together?"

Carl Craven Clammer hated being called Clam Man. "For what?"

"A counter-counterintelligence paramilitary operation... someone in the intelligence community is working a project without our knowledge and they might be the ones who killed our cooperating tech gurus.

"I thought that was a murder suicide."

"Sorry... Assassination. Probably by someone involved in the US military or intelligence."

"Shit... any ideas?"

"My best guess is that it's a team of cowboys put together by you know who. I'm mean what the hell, does he think he's Teddy Roosevelt or something?"

"Shit."

"What can you do?"

"I don't know. We should await orders."

"No time… we have to deal with this or it's our ass."

"Let me think. I'll call you tomorrow."

The FBI director disconnected. *Can the CIA Director be trusted to be loyal to their Chinese benefactors?* The bastard was already up to his ears serving Iranian interests. The son of a bitch might as well have business cards that say '*Have Treason. Will Travel.*' The FBI man decided that he might have to have the CIA Director killed later. Nobody liked the son of a bitch anyway. But for now, he remained necessary to the cause.

## THE TOWER OF KONA RESORT HOTEL- HAWAII

Mac tried to get the typically stoic and quiet old man to have a conversation with him. "What are you carrying?"

"I decided to step it up a notch. Standard NVGs, comm pack, an M4, and my old Kimber Classic 1911. How about you?"

"NVGs, comms, an M249, an AK47, a 590 Shockwave SPX, a good morning sunshine bag, two Glock 17s, two Glock 26s, a claymore, two *more* 17s, a Glock compatible folding Sub2K converted to select fire with four drum magazines and thirty happy sticks... and my lucky helmet... oh, and my EDC Ruger."

The old man shook his head in disbelief... but still, he'd seen his lumbering partner carry that loadout before, so he knew he was serious. "I'm glad you're carrying all that shit and not me. No primary weapon?"

"No... I left it in storage on the plane. This project didn't seem to be that big a deal. Besides, we still have five more of these guru knobs to whack after this one and at least one of those jobs has to look like an accident."

"Very thoughtful of you. You're a real team player... for a worthless dickwad."

The combination compliment-insult slid off his back. "Thanks. So now what scenario are we using for this?"

"I'm leaning towards kill all the Chinese guys, kill everyone in the house, and let the police sort it out. When you have forty or fifty heavily armed foreign dead guys at the scene, it's often difficult to determine who is to blame. The bigger the mess, the less the cops care about details. I think if we let Deeter's PR crew drop some media stories that this is all China's fault and they will completely forget about little old us."

Mac liked it. "That's simply good common sense, right there. I agree."

Pearson added, "*And*, it might give our head guy a good excuse to nuke those commie maggots." Pearson added with a rare smile-like expression.

Mac snickered. "Like he needs one."

Both men shared a good laugh at that inside joke.

Pearson finished organizing his gear and gave the order, "We roll in two hours. Time to kill a commie for mommy."

Mac put a hand on Pearson's shoulder and smiled warmly. "You had me at *kill*."

Pearson gave him the finger. "Fuck you, hippy."

Mac wondered why it was that the more deeply Pearson got involved in a nasty-assed blood and guts suicide mission, the more human he became. What a guy.

Pearson added, "I'll call Deeter and see if he can get an island-wide power outage arranged for 2200 hours."

"Copy that."

"And by the way, what the fuck is a good morning sunshine bag?"

"Some might call it a master key; others might like to call it an all-access pass... I like to call it a fifty-pound satchel charge of C4 stuffed with miscellaneous hardware parts and fishing tackle."

"Damned right, *good morning*! That will come in handy."

"Exactly."

## NIGHTFALL IN HAWAII

Conditions were as good as one could hope for, overcast, a slight drizzle, fog, and almost no moon. With the advantage of the latest technology night vision goggles, the two men silently made their way through the jungle as though it was noon on a sunny day, and they were invisible.

They found the gate again and waited. Assuming there were ground-sensors and heat detectors placed on the estate grounds, the only opportunity for surprise was in the initial contact. It was ten minutes before the scheduled power shutdown, and they were in position.

Mac heard one word whispered in his ear comm. "Go."

Sneaking past random patrolling guards, Mac crept in closer to the same gate they tried before. It was a suitable location, as it seemed to still be dense with enemy defenders.

This time he was prepared to pay these commie scumbags a visit. He placed the detonator in the C4 and left the satchel charge near the starboard side hinges of the twenty-foot-wide iron gates. He slowly began crab walking back to his assigned position when he flattened himself on the ground. A guard walked directly towards him. He remained as still as possible.

In darkness, it's easy to assume someone sees you but if you are motionless, there is a good chance that you remain invisible to observation. At least that's what Mac learned in training. Right now, Mac hoped that was true. The guard ambled by without incident.

Mac continued to crawl back into position.

He touched his comm unit. "Sunshine is in place. Morning comes in one minute."

He heard two quick squelches in his earpiece... he unslung the M249, charged it, and jammed an unlit Lucky in his mouth. It was time to do some bad ass shit... American shit... for America.... hell yeah!

Then the sky lit up.

## FEATHERSTON ESTATE — HAWAII - INSIDE THE MAIN HOUSE

Devin Featherston twirled around in panic as all the windows on the east side of the house exploded inward, the ground shook, and fire scorched the sky turning it into a crimson and orange modern art piece. *What the hell just happened? Was that a volcano erupting?*

Those rude men, the strangers who had taken over his home against his orders, were sprinting for the exits with automatic weapons, establishing a defensive perimeter in the house. There were many more of them than he had realized. Their rapid movement and precision actions appeared to be coordinated. It looked like they had practiced it. *When did they practice this? Why would they practice this?* Then he heard gunfire and men screaming outside.

This was worse than any video game he had ever played. He peed his pants a little. Suddenly, he squeaked as he felt a powerful hand grab his forearm and drag him toward the basement stairwell. It was his wife... but she seemed different... stronger... dangerous.

## Featherston Estate - The Main Gate

Every security operator in the immediate vicinity of the gate was dead, killed by the satchel charge blast, which Mac thought, might have been overkill... if there was such a thing as overkill. He counted at least twenty bodies, or at least there appeared to be enough parts strewn about to make twenty bodies. In retrospect, throwing a few boxes of 16D common nails and #10 sheet metal screws in the bag with a couple of dozen bass fishing lures probably wasn't necessary, but it *did* make an awful mess. Those particular commie maggots wouldn't be sticking their noses into America's business again.

Mac heard a triple squelch sound. Pearson was ready to move in. Mac quick peeked over his shoulder and spotted him. He gave a hand signal indicating his intent to advance and led the way.

They moved tactically moved through the gate, using cover and concealment as they advanced onto a narrow dirt road, maybe better described as a jeep trail, winding through dense tropical foliage. Mac saw Pearson move to the edge of the road and kneel along the side. He gave another hand signal. It was time to move off the road and make way through the trees and brush.

Spotting an almost imperceptible movement, Mac raised a fist. Pearson stopped.

"Sniper at 2 o'clock," he whispered into his comm unit.

Pearson responded, "I see him, stand by."

Mac heard the deadly whisper of the suppressed M4 and then watched as a Chinese marksman and a rifle dropped from a tree stand, splatting onto the dirt with a dull thud. The body didn't have much of a face. Pearson caught him right in the center of his nose with a frangible round.

Mac heard Pearson's voice in his ear comm again.

"You owe me a beer, you pussy."

It looked like Pearson was smiling. Murder always brought out the best in him.

## FEATHERSTON ESTATE - INSIDE THE MAIN HOUSE

Featherston was nearing a state of shock... running was uncomfortable. His wife held a vice-like grip on his arm as she pulled him down the stairs into the security bunker. He noticed she had a firearm in her hand... what the hell was that about? She had been telling him for years that firearms should be banned, they should never be kept in the home, and that firearm owners were evil... She was shouting orders to the men in Chinese... what the hell was going on?

Featherston felt fear pulsing through his veins, cold stark fear. He raged internally as he stood by helplessly. *I'm a CEO. I'm in charge here, I want answers,* he thought as he tried to stir up enough courage to confront his wife. Finally, he dug in his heels. He shouted at her in voice that projected all the command presence of a petulant toddler. "What is this? I want to call the police! What's wrong with you? Stop this right now!"

Her back to him, she froze at his words. Spinning around into a low martial arts stance with an almost imperceptible flash of speed, his wife punched him in the nuts with a vicious left uppercut.

"Iyahhh!" she screamed as she used fa sheng to generate maximum power into the strike.

"My balls!" he squealed back in a high-pitched rasp.

He collapsed on his knees, feeling like he might puke. He hadn't been punched in the gonads since the fourth grade. It hurt then… it hurt like hell now. *Getting punched in the balls isn't a good thing*, he thought.

She muttered a curse in Chinese, grabbed him by the collar, and roughly dragged him down the stairs like a sack of potatoes.

Despite the pain he was now consumed with outraged. He wanted to fight… but he was afraid…

*I'm a pussy*, he thought as he mentally surrendered his manhood to the will of his violent and frightening wife... all four-foot-eleven of her.

It was time to go with the flow.

## FEATHERSTON ESTATE GROUNDS

"This place is crawling with commies," Mac complained as he reloaded while Pearson provided cover.

They both crawled to good cover and disappeared into the dark green foliage.

Mac's voice came through Pearson's ear comm. "Yeah, it's a little more than I expected, but that's show biz."

"What is?" Pearson was a little annoyed. That dipshit was always saying stuff that made little sense.

Mac didn't understand the question, "Huh?"

Pearson tried to keep him focused. "Never mind. It looks like most of them are falling back to the main house and establishing a fortified defensive position. We're going to have to take it down the hard way."

"So, what we have been doing so far is the *easy way*? Because I don't think I'm going to like the hard way," Mac groused. Complaining might annoy others, but it *is* free... and if good old Benito 'Mac'

McCartney was anything, it was frugal. Bitching to Pearson was a real bargain.

Pearson ignored Mac's whining and popped a running Chinese operative in the back of the head at one hundred and fifty yards, "Suck it up for Bluffton, maggot," he muttered as he mentally added one to the body count stats in his head.

"Who?" Mac asked as he looked for targets.

Pearson spotted another one behind concealment. *Pop*... and dead. He returned his attention to Mac's question and elaborated, "Bluffton is where I went to college and played football. 'Suck it up for Bluffton' is a figure of speech that only manly men use. You wouldn't know anything about it, pussy."

"Oh." Mac responded curtly. The old man was always calling him a pussy. Which Mac found annoying and somewhat rude. But he was old, a total badass, and still alive, so he had the legal right to call everybody a puss.

The old man scolded him, "Now shut up, we got to earn our keep."

Mac crept up on an operative who was focusing on firing a round into Pearson. The man was stretched out under a fern, looking down the barrel of what looked like a commie version of an MP5... probably a piece of shit knock-off weapon.

Mac smiled, the dumbass under the fern was so focused on killing Pearson that he failed to notice Mac.

Mac lunged in an extended leap with his arms outstretched like he was jumping off a diving board. His knife was clutched in his hands. He came down with his full massive body weight on the operative's back and buried the blade into the back of the man's head so deeply the point of the knife stuck out from between the commie's eyes.

He whispered in the dead man's ear before he got up, providing free advice that was no longer really needed. "Never wait too long to shoot a guy... because there is always another guy you didn't know about waiting to kill you... dumbass."

The dead guy didn't respond. Mac placed both of his feet on the sides of the guy's head and yanked his knife out of the dead man's skull... It was still early. He might need it again before the evening's project was over.

"Where are you?" Pearson asked over the comm.

"Sorry. I had to kill a guy," Mac responded, not disclosing that his aggressive actions had just saved Pearson's life.

"Quit messing around and get over here."

Mac crawled across the ground to a position beside the old man. "Now what?"

"It's time to step it up a notch."

The pair suspected that all the operatives had fallen back to the main house. Pearson said what they were both thinking, "Gas main leak?"

Mac smiled, but then frowned, "I don't think they have gas lines out here."

"Do you think anyone will mention that?"

"Probably not… everybody hates this turd."

"We just need another bomb."

Mac hesitantly spoke, "I wasn't going to mention it, since you get so weird about this whole '*make it look like an accident*' thing but got another bomb back at the hotel." Mac made finger quotes when he said *make it look like an accident.*

The update pissed the old man off. "How in the hell does *that* help? It will take you over an hour to get there and back."

Mac shrugged. "I'll hurry."

Pearson issued a stink eye.

Mac tried again. "I'll be very hurrier up… most riki-tik…" He attempted to talk like the old Vietnam vet did around his friends in a flimsy attempt to win him over to the idea.

"Fine," the old man said. "I'll keep these commie fuckers busy until then. Hey," he added, "do you still have that claymore?"

"Yeah." Mac was surprised his negotiating ploy worked. As ploys go, even Mac thought his idea was stupid. *You never know with this old fart knocker*, he thought.

"Give it to me."

McCartney dug into his gear bag and fished out the claymore.

Pearson shoved it in his rucksack. "Thanks… now haul ass, you pussy. I can't hang around here all day waiting on you."

The old man watched as Mac crawled back and away from the scene.

Finally, he thought. I can let my hair down and have some fun.

# Chapter 6 – Never piss off an unsupervised senior citizen with a gun

FEATHERSTON ESTATE - HAWAII

Pearson swept the perimeter, seeking out any stragglers before he assaulted the mansion full of highly trained commie assholes. He knew that although it appeared as though they all fell back to the house, there would still be some residual ambushers deployed on the grounds. He slid his Ka Bar out of the sheath and crawled over to a small outbuilding that seemed to be a good place to look for maggots.

Pearson pressed his ear against the side of the building. He could hear movement. Frowning, he began experiencing doubts about these guys being as good as he originally thought.

He noted that the little eight by ten building had one door and one window both on the same side. That would make it difficult to go in and stab everyone with his knife, which in a perfect world would be the way he preferred to kill commies. He reached into a pocket to retrieve a grenade when he realized he didn't have a grenade.

He found a medium-sized rock on the ground nearby, threw it through the window, and shouted, *"Shǒuliúdàn"* ... which he thought might be Mandarin for grenade.

Two operators dove out through the doorway.

Pearson jumped on the closest one and stabbed him twice in the neck, driving the blade of the big Marine fighting knife almost up to the hilt.

The other, realizing what happened and seeing his comrade nearly decapitated, instinctively jumped on Pearson's back.

Pearson was not much of a martial arts man. He had extensive training in all the fancy stuff, but his preference was alley fighting. He reached back and crushed his attackers nuts, then shrugged him off to the side, got to his feet, and throat stomped him.

He crawled away to the next target. Typically, defenders place the most resources at the point they expect to be attacked, or if they have no clue, they put the bulk of their power at the front. Pearson carefully placed the claymore against a tree at eye level facing the front of the house. He placed the remote detonator in his front shirt pocket. A little something to look forward too later.

Moving deeper into the brush, he retrieved his monocular from a pocket and slowly glassed the area. He found ambushers in under two minutes... a pair of clowns with a frigging belt-fed machine gun set up about thirty yards away. Annoying bastards. They looked nervous, but most people do when they hear someone shouting in their vicinity about hand grenades. Pearson went back to the knife.

He made his way to the rear of the two defenders and paused. They had a radio... perfect.

He creeped up silently, knife in hand. He got within three feet when the first one noticed his presence and reacted. The man rolled on his back and reached for a sidearm.

Pearson pounced, jamming the knife blade deep into his throat while simultaneously dropping a knee into the small of the back of the other man. He pulled the knife out of newly-dead-guy one and repeatedly stabbed soon-to-be-dead-guy two.

He rolled them away and took the radio. He keyed the mike and broadcasted a general message in his deep resonate voice, "This is the Supreme Commander of United Nations Forces. We have an overwhelming force of five hundred soldiers and... a tank... two tanks. We will give you ten minutes to prepare for your deaths. That is all."

He hoped that while they translated that load of total bullshit into Chinese, it would buy more time for

Mac to get back with the bomb. In the meantime, he would plan to launch his attack in eight minutes. There couldn't be over fifty of them left.

## LAKE TEKAPO - SOUTH ISLAND, GOLDBURN'S NEW ZEALAND ESTATE

Despite controlling the Web's most popular video browser, advertising businesses, news media outlets, and the premier marketing intelligence organization, Gary Graham Goldburn was oblivious to the emerging threat of Washington-based treachery.

Goldburn's cooperation with the deep state was a well-guarded secret. His company compiled files on every citizen of the United States and most of the world population. Although his reputation as a business genius was renowned, what wasn't as well-known was his early Chinese financial backing. Communist backers who maintained a team of experts at the top tier of every element of his business. Goldburn, often described by his peers as an awkward wimp of a man desperately wanting to be macho, believed the Chinese intelligence agents were part of his loyal start-up team and an innocent part of the family of corporations he owned. He had no idea his surreptitious relationship with China was fueling an imminent demise of Western Civilization.

In addition to Goldburn's private security force and team of hired mercenaries, the Chinese had their own security force in play. Typically, over one-hundred members of elite Chinese soldiers were assigned in covert roles about the estate to protect his interests in the company.

Goldburn also gladly accepted additional secret 'partnerships' with Iran and Russia. He was an equal opportunity traitor. Anything they needed on US citizens was sold at a discounted price.

His so-called partners suspected, but were not convinced, of each the other's relationship with the greedy tech entrepreneur… a tangled web of corruption wrapped in a thick veil of superciliousness.

Goldburn believed that his competing associations would no longer be an issue when the exterminations began, so the gamble didn't appear to present an unreasonable risk. Besides, he was more than prepared militarily to defend his secret home base in addition to executing his clever under the table deals.

Between staff, security, and Goldburn's immediate entourage, the force outnumbered the population of the village in the valley below them.

Goldburn selected this location as his home base for the group's mass extermination plan. It was perfect. No matter what kind of pandemic weapon they might use to wipe out the bulk of the world's unnecessary population, the weapon would spare the immediate population. The northern island would, of course, be depopulated. Those people were not of use.

Goldburn, wearing his satin bikini shorts and silk slippers, relaxed in his Luraco i7 iRobotics massage chair, gazing out the twelve-foot-wide floor-to-ceiling bulletproof window that provided his exquisite view of the lake. Perfection, he thought. Hydro-electric power, isolation, a local population that could serve any purposes he deemed necessary, local food supplies, a small airport, and generally mild weather year around. The best part was, nobody can do anything about it, he pondered. His vast wealth bought huge swaths of land. His political savvy had placed extremely weak-minded politicians in charge of the government that allowed him to petition to close the military training base located nearby and have it 'licensed' to his company for security training. One constable, who he owned, was the sole security for miles. Once the plan for he would start the process to make the rest of the small island country his own.

Life is good in New Zealand, he thought… then smirked, at least for me it is... as soon as I get all these sheep humping locals off my island.

## FEATHERSTON ESTATE - HAWAII

Pearson found a shallow ravine twenty yards behind the house. He could see men stationed at nearly every window and door. What the men didn't know was that about seven hundred ball bearings would fly into the main building from a claymore positioned five feet off the ground in the front of the house. Pearson believed that would make them sad. But mass murder didn't trouble him much. *If the tables were turned, these bastards would do far worse to me, so tough shit, he thought.*

He looked around for McCartney. Nothing…

*You better get your sorry ass back here soon, kid*, he thought as he hit the remote detonator switch, not wanting Mac to miss out on all the fun.

Pearson ducked down into the ravine as far as he could as the explosive sound of the claymore detonation shook his world.

The old man laughed to himself as he heard the death screams of dozens of Chinese operatives, punctured, mutilated, and disemboweled, suffering their painful demise in the aftermath of the initial blast. An old thought taught to him by his father, a Korean war vet came to mind… *Commies aren't real people.*

He found a hand grenade and tossed it into the mess that used to be a mansion. He heard even more screaming as the house began filling up with the dense black smoke of a hot fire while the occupants choked on the life-stealing toxic stench of burning furniture and goods.

The old man clutched his M4 and charged in through the remains of the front door, diving into the room like a suicidal maniac. In the smoky confusion, he spotted a man on his back clambering for a weapon just outside his reach. Pearson shot him in the dick. Instead of reaching for the weapon, the man now grabbed the area where his wanker used to be and began rolling on the floor screaming in pain and despair.

Pearson growled, "Walk it off, pussy!"

A large man in a black suit racked a round into the chamber of a twelve-gauge pump shotgun. With two near simultaneous trigger pulls, Pearson shot him in the right eye and in the forehead. Neutralized. The old man spit on shotgun dude's body as he briskly walked by on the way to kill more people.

Two more came out of a room to Pearson's right, firing sub-machine guns as they moved on his position.

A round caught Pearson in the shoulder. He fell backwards on his ass, but instinctively switched his weapon to the other hands and gut shot both men. The first man he hit took the bullet dead center in the solar plexus. It exited a lung, causing him to suck wind and spit blood. The second man took a round lower in the belly, destroying important bodily function stuff like a bladder and lower intestine. The man quit fighting and fell on the floor moaning.

Pearson got to his feet again, walked over to the two men, pulled his custom 1911, and shot them both in the head. "Not what I had in mind when I asked for the senior citizen discount, assholes."

Across the room, the man Pearson previously shot in the groin moaned, "What do you mean? What are you asking for? I need a doctor."

Pearson turned toward him and made eye contact. "Sorry, I forgot you were there." The old man shot him in the head twice. The two forty-five caliber, two-hundred-and-forty grain hollow points took a shitload of skull and brains off the top of the questioner's melon. Pearson snickered. *I probably did him a favor,* he thought. *Puss.*

He paused long enough to reload and then fill his shoulder wound up with some quick clotting powder. He slapped on an adhesive patch... not great but still not bad for a field combat repair. He gave himself an injection of something that he had custom designed a few years back made of adrenalin and a potent painkiller. *Coffee break is over, time to get to work.*

He avoided going upstairs, instead choosing to look for the basement access. He had a nerd to smoke… and probably some more goddamned commies too.

He moved into the kitchen and around to the vault-like door in the pantry… it was the secret access door to the basement, but it looked more like a bank vault.

A footstep.

Pearson dove for cover and rolled on his back, ready to put a shit-ton of rounds downrange.

A voice came from the smoky kitchen, "Looks like somebody could use some explodey stuff…"

It was Mac.

The old man muttered, "You dick! I almost killed your ass."

"Sorry old-timer, did I startle you?" He suddenly detected the old man's wounds. "Uh oh… somebody got a boo-boo."

Pearson scowled. "Shut your pie hole and make me a doorway, asshole. I can't wait all day on your stupid-assed kid shit."

"Ask nicely!" Mac said as he started setting a charge.

Veins in Pearson's forehead started visibly pulsing. "Fuck you."

Mac refused to react to Pearson's profanity. "Close enough. I accept your apology." Mac placed some of the C4 and detonator on the door. They retreated to the front of the house.

The old man whispered, "After we pop this metal door, put on your NVGs… it's going to be dark down there…"

"Copy that."

The explosion rocked the house, almost bringing it down on top of them. Mac laughed… and coughed on the dust… and sneezed. "Cool."

The old man couldn't help but smile too… even after all these years, blowing shit up is still awesome, he thought.

They could hear screaming, shouting, and cries of panic coming from the basement.

Pearson grinned a rare grin. "I think we got their attention."

"Let's go." Mac pulled on his seventh generation NVGs and headed for the door. The night vision device looked like wrap-around sports sunglasses providing enhanced daylight and darkness vision, constantly adjusting to conditions. Suddenly, the floor trembled so severely, he almost fell over.

New explosions from outside the house shook the ground like a 7.0 earthquake.

"What the hell is that?" Pearson asked, holding on to a countertop with one hand as he tried to get his NVGs on with the other.

"Oh, I forgot to tell you, when I was coming back, I launched a surveillance drone… they got three big ass commie tanks at the beach… they're probably trying to kill us."

"Shit… show me…"

More explosions shook the living shit out of them like a rat in a dog's mouth. They huddled up between the deafening booms.

Mac pushed a button on his high-tech communication and surveillance band on his right arm and a photo from the drone appeared on the flexible flat panel screen.

Pearson didn't like what he saw. "Fuck me… those are Boyevaya Mashina Fourteens…"

"What the hell is that in English?"

"Big fucking commie tanks."

Mac frowned, "I hate tanks… when somebody else has them… otherwise I like them," Mac elaborated pointlessly. "You know… because… tanks…"

"Exactly... you're not as stupid as you look kid."

"Thanks, I appreciate that," Mac said with a wide Labrador Retriever-like smile.

The old man flipped him the finger, "Fuck you, I was lying." *Idiot has no grasp of sarcasm,* he thought.

"Still… it's the words that count," Mac said solemnly.

"Thoughts."

"About what?"

"No... stupid, it's the *thought* that... never mind... let's kill these commie spank-weasels before they croak from old age."

The pair stacked and moved toward the gaping black hole that used to be the entrance. Mac could see the twisted metal remnants of the door at the bottom of where the staircase used to be. It led to a wall then took a hard right. They would have to go in blind.

The drop was about twelve feet. They both hopped down into the wreckage, guns at the ready.

The dust in the sub-level was dense in the air. The building continued shaking from the tank barrage.

Mac and Pearson stacked and moved through the maze of debris, shooting anything that moved, wiggled, or twitched.

Resistance was minimal.

Mac raised a closed fist, stopped, and pointed. "What do you think that is?" he asked, spotting another doorway at the back of the basement.

Pearson answered with his best guess. "Probably their safe room. That's probably where we'll find our missing asshole."

"Moving!"

Pearson advanced to the left side of the door. Mac took a position on the right. Plaster and debris shook down from the ceiling as the tanks continued to drop HE rounds around the perimeter of the house.

The musty smell of the dirt and dust filled their nostrils. Mac pulled his bandana up over his nose.

Mac sneezed twice and muttered, "This shit sucks."

Pearson ignored Mac's complaint. "We've got to crack this hatch."

Mac tried the doorknob. The door came open an inch.

"Shitty safe room," Mac commented.

"Only if you forget to lock the door." Pearson put a size eleven boot to the door, slamming it wide open.

In the darkness were two figures.

An Asian woman held a semi-automatic handgun to the head of a tall freckle-faced skinny dweeb. "Move and I'll kill this gutless little prick," she stuck her head out and snarled menacingly as she held the scrawny computer guru in front of her for cover.

Mac shot her in the mouth. She dropped like a damp dishrag into a lifeless heap on the floor.

A confused Devin Featherston pissed himself. "You shot my wife, you bastards."

Mac unslung the 590 Shockwave from his kit. "Yes, I believe that *was* us… sorry."

"I'm not." Pearson said. Something is wrong here. Why is this little bastard pissed about having his commie tormentor shot?

Featherston, not particularly skilled as assessing dangerous situations, pressed the matter. Now mistakenly believing that the two operators were not there to kill him, but instead were on some sort of misguided rescue mission, he felt safe enough to bluster. "I'll sue you both into the stone age. You Neanderthals have no right to invade my estate. I'm one of the greatest men in the world…. Do you even know who I am?"

Pearson used that question to seek clarity. "Are you Devin Featherston?"

"Damn right I am," he spat out defiantly with his bony shoulders thrust back and his peach fuzz covered chin tilted up.

Pearson delivered his follow up question. "The FacePlace guy?"

"Yes, I *am* FacePlace…" he said indignantly, "the greatest social media interface in the history of the world. I literally control *thought* across this planet… I control every discussion on earth. I control elections, I control everything, including you, you filthy brutes!"

Pearson glanced over at his partner. "All yours, Mac."

Mac jacked a round in the 590 and emptied a load of twelve-gauge double-aught buck into Featherston's chest and another into the side his head turning him into a fairly decent imitation of ground beef from the waist up. The dead guru fell flat onto his back, spread-eagled on the floor.

Pearson snapped his 1911 out of the holster in an amazingly fast quickdraw and put one more in Featherston's head just for good measure. One and a half seconds from the moment the .45 broke leather, the old government model was back in the holster

Mac did a double take, still amazed at the old man's speed, before commenting on the coup de grâce, "Nice... I hate FacePlace. I've been banned like six times already."

Already occupied with the next task, Pearson ignored him. *The locals will love us forever for this next shit*, he thought as he considered the best way to burn the estate buildings to the ground.

## WASHINGTON DC

The National Security Advisor scrambled into the President's working office with a document clutched in his shaking hand. Gasping from the sprint down the hall, he breathlessly blurted out the latest *crisis*, "Mr. President... something terrible has happened."

The President, who often worked late into the night, briefly looked up from the financial report he received earlier from the Department of Commerce. "Calm down and take a deep breath... what's up?"

The Advisor took a deep breath and handed the report to the President as he spoke, "Three major tech CEOs have died in the past week. They just now found Featherston from FacePlace burned to death in some kind of... mysterious fire at his Hawaiian mansion. They're saying it's a gas leak but there were bodies found at the scene... Chinese bodies!"

Nonplussed, the President of the United States responded by handing the report back and returning to his stack of paperwork. "Sad... send flowers."

# Chapter 7 – Never piss off an asshole with a gun

At one in the morning eastern daylight time, CIA Director Clammer called the FBI Director.

In three rings the head of the Bureau answered with a sleepy hello.

The Director of Central Intelligence blurted out his words with the same desperation as a first grader making an announcement that he desperately has to pee. "This is Clammer… they're killing more of the tech guys."

"*Who* is doing *what*?" the blast of information confused the Director of Federal Bureau of Investigations.

Clammer knew he sounded like he was in full freak out mode. But he was in full freak out mode. "I don't know…" he grumbled, knowing his attempt to conceal his near panic state failed miserably.

"You're the head of the CIA, Carl… what do you mean you don't know?" the FBI director asked accusingly, despite his not knowing either.

Clammer sucked it up and prattled on, "All I know is all hell is breaking loose in Hawaii. Now, in addition to the two dead tech guys in Los Angeles we have a shit show in Paradise. I think the assholes who wiped out Hawaii are the same assholes killed the two guys in Los Angeles… that's no coincidence. They didn't go to New Zealand like we thought… they hit us here in the States again."

"Hawaii?" The FBI Director was still confused. "Assholes… What assholes?"

"Yes, they took out Featherston. There must have been a battalion of special forces to pull that off. And there were acres of dead Chinese operatives at the scene. It's the most horrendous display of mayhem I've ever witnessed. I almost puked. I'm going to go to counseling. It was awful."

"You went there?"

"Well, I mean I looked at the pictures. It was awful… Bodies everywhere. Dead bodies."

The leader of the FBI did an eye roll. "Oh… I am sorry you had to endure that, Clam Man," he responded condescendingly. *You puss*, he thought.

The disrespectful tone didn't deter Clammer. "It doesn't matter where I was… this level of violence must involve some rogue element of the Army… I can't believe they are loyal to the country… I mean the President… whatever… they're not following our playbook. We set national security policy… they need to follow it. Otherwise how do we make money?" Clammer openly voiced his disdain for the commander-in-chief in the name of American patriotism but remained an active yet covert communist party member. And of course, having an amazingly comfortable lifestyle funded by the Chinese and the Mullahs he served on the side was nice… and none of those assholes were fans of the President either. "I think we might be in deep shit."

The FBI Director agreed with Clammer's assessment. His personal stake was similar. "I *know*, right?" he commiserated.

"We have to stop them," Clammer declared.

"How?"

"Send more men?" Clammer suggested in the form of a question asked like a nine-year-old caught flat-footed not paying attention in class.

"Where?" The FBI Director asked. "If we had more men, where the hell would we send them?"

Clammer explained, "I suspect they'll go after Goldburn next in New Zealand."

"Who?" the FBI director, who was a sleazy Washington DC attorney by trade, was confused. After all, he wasn't a *real* cop *or* a *real* spy. His law degree and honest face tended to provide him with more credit than he deserved from the public, who mistakenly thought he was an intelligent and well-read man instead of a half-wit frat boy past his prime.

"Goldburn… CEO of Brazilo and every search engine on the planet," Clammer explained, exasperated with his half-wit counterpart. *You'd think this clown would be smarter*, he thought.

"The tech guy who also owns the newspaper?"

"Yes… *that* asshole."

"The guy who we leak information on the administration too?"

"Yes… *that* is the asshole…" Clammer's frustration with the man who was the face of the FBI was evident in his voice.

"Where?"

"New Zealand." Clammer repeated.

"Isn't that part of Australia?"

"No… it's a country… I don't know… it's in the South Pacific." Clammer really didn't know where or what it was but it sounded familiar.

"Shit."

"Right?"

The FBI director hesitantly asked, "So, where can we get more fighters?"

"I can get another two-hundred mercenaries from Myanmar."

"Is that Burma?" The FBI man asked, unsure of where or what it was… but it sounded familiar. He read about the country being renamed for some reason.

"Yeah, same thing… basically a conglomeration of warlords with military forces equal to, if not superior to, a lot of nation states. There's a War Lord there in the Shan State who owes me a big favor," Clammer offered not revealing the name of Weng Lo Lew.

"A favor for what?"

"Don't ask." Clammer didn't want this nitwit launching a criminal investigation. The head of the FBI could not be trusted by anyone… even his fellow traitors.

The FBI Director was desperate… *if this flip of the tech community continues; I stand to lose millions… millions and go to jail… both of those things. Shit*! He blathered out a limited approval. "Then send them… but don't let Goldburn know… keep them on the perimeter in case his security fails. The less anybody knows, the better."

Clammer pointlessly whispered in a conspiratorial tone, "In that case we shouldn't leave anyone who can testify against us if the tech group's initiative fails. Someone is on to it. We don't know who or why or what. We don't know jack shit. Our exposure is immeasurable."

The Director of the FBI couldn't disagree. If the world found out what they had been up to in collusion with the tech gurus, they would all hang. "I agree. Let's terminate this fiasco in New Zealand. And by terminate, I mean scorched earth. Can the Burmese guys be traced back to us in any way?"

"Never…. They are the most ruthless bastards who have ever lived but if they give their word on a debt, they won't renege… they have some kind of stupid ass code of honor. Very violent people, but they won't screw us."

"Do it." The director disconnected the call then muttered to himself, "Asshole…"

Clammer put his phone back in his pocket. "Asshole…"

## New York City – CNT World News Broadcasting

Newsreader Jennifer Calbado smiled as she thought, *this broadcast will totally bump my rating numbers*. Her desperation to beat Tom Rucker's competing cable news show was palpable. She despised the man since he declared that her network hired only ugly women, although she self-identified as a non-binary attractive being… still… the insult enraged her. She believed her man-like haircut, her man-like suit, and her oversized glasses made her beautiful in her own way. And this crummy hack from Fax News, who attended some podunk midwestern state university, had the nerve to insult *her*… a graduate of *Brown*… a *Rhodes Scholar*… An anchorperson on *Central News Television*… it was unacceptable.

The make-up crew did the best with what they had to work with, and the director did a hand signal countdown giving her the signal to begin reading the teleprompter out loud.

*I'm so good at this shit*, she thought… she started reading. "Tonight, in Hawaii, tragic news as technology Icon Devin Featherston and his devoted wife were killed at their tropical retreat in a freak gas line explosion. They were hosting a peace delegation of diplomats from the People's Republic of China when an experimental clean energy environmentally friendly natural gas fuel line he was designing to help impoverished developing nations, accidently exploded, leveling the massive coastal estate. Our nation is saddened at the loss of one of our greatest creators, leaders, patriots, and heroes."

On cue, the station cut to a montage of Featherston and his wife set to sad elevator music… mostly shots of them posing… Like posers… each photograph about as authentic as perfectly staged smiling baby photos.

The montage cross faded back into the studio with Jennifer sitting behind the desk. She bit down into the little piece of onion she had been hiding in her desk drawer. It worked. Her eyes moistened... *perfect, I look like I give a shit about this nerd,* she thought as she delivered her last line of the broadcast.

"And tonight." She paused for dramatic effect. "America mourns."

The director gave commands. "Fade to black. Cue commercial. Aaaand cut."

Jennifer grinned widely. She nailed her slam dunk report... *Suck it Rucker! Emmy time!*

## LAKE TEKAPO - SOUTH ISLAND, NEW ZEALAND HILLSIDE

The Myanmar commandos deployed from the Shan State by their War Lord Weng Lo Lew, secretly arrived on the far side of the island without notice. They began setting up covert observation posts, hiding deep in the craggy hills high above the vast mountain estate of their target, Gary Graham Goldburn, the tech mega-billionaire and conspirator.

Within two days, the insertion was complete and undetected, executed with top tier special operations skills. Their forces remained unobserved by the resident security staff as they spread through the property like an infectious disease.

## BEIJING CHINA

The powerful and ruthless Deputy Chairman Zhao lit a cigarette as he reviewed the encrypted email. *So, the final stage is close*, he thought. The key tech guru, the one who stayed off the radar was close to the breakthrough and they virus would soon be ready to deploy.

He took a deep drag on his Chunghwa brand smoke. *While every one of these entitled capitalist swine works so hard to become the final elite of earth, they have no idea I control their labs. I control the research. I control their people. Soon the virus will kill every white, black, and brown person on earth… and the world will belong to its rightful heirs, the Peoples' Republic of China.*

The failed Coronavirus outbreak in Wuhan was supposed to be the final test to prove Chinese DNA was immune to the bioweapon. But the test failed and nearly caused a pandemic resulting in severe damage to Zhao's standing in the party. Only his history of success at all costs provided him with another opportunity.

He smiled. *This time though, with the help of our agents among the Canadian and US researchers, we have it.*

He slowly exhaled a smoke ring that floated awkwardly toward the ceiling, almost amorphous. Zhao reflected, *if you expect to see a ring, it will always look like a ring. And if Americans expect to see reasonable negotiations and cooperation, that is what they will see. As soon as the last ounce of national treasure is wrung out of the western countries, the virus will be released, and the bastards will die by the billions. And their own security and technology apparatus is the murder weapon.*

Zhao ground the butt out in a golden ashtray and went to bed.

## WASHINGTON D.C.

The President touched a button on the intercom and gave orders for his son to report to the Oval Office. A secret service agent escorted Deeter from down the hall, through the door, and to the Resolute Desk.

The President looked up from his reading. "Son... Glad you are back. How are things going with the mission?"

Deeter smiled. "Good, Mr. President. Messy, but good."

"That doesn't surprise me. We give them assignments of extreme risk... some of the most extreme risks of any risk ever seen before. Very extreme. Very extreme... But we can't expect them to walk on eggshells out there, that I can tell you."

The President's son stayed on point. "Any updates from our source?"

"Just that something is up... and it possibly involves the CIA and the FBI."

"Not surprising. We must clean those rat holes out. Our officers and agents deserve better. Second term priority?"

The President smiled. "Yes... but we can start now. Get Bill on the phone and see if he is available for lunch. He's going to be busy with the Federal Grand Jury. It's time we launch phase two of our little swamp draining party."

## LAKE TEKAPO - SOUTH ISLAND, NEW ZEALAND ESTATE

The normally cocky CEO of tech conglomerate Brazilo fought the urge to shit his pants as he watched the news broadcasts of what was being called *The Hawaiian Disaster*.

"Bullshit!" he yelled out loud although no one was in the room with him.

The head of his personal security force was watching the news reports from his desk in the hallway outside the CEO's office, when heard his boss swearing. He entered the futuristic office suite and tried in vain to talk his boss down. "Sir... They're saying it was a gas leak, Mr. Goldburn. We can't jump to conclusions here. I'll look into it further and..."

The CEO wasn't having it and cut him off. "Bullshit... A gas explosion never happened... This was a military hit." Goldburn argued. "What the hell are you doing about it?"

The security director didn't disagree. "We'll adjust appropriately, sir."

## Lake Tekapo - South Island, The ridgeline above the New Zealand Estate

Colonel Ko was in a reasonably upbeat mood for a murdering psychopath. Infiltrating the estate was almost too easy. Chinese arrogance was working to his advantage. The mercenary force protecting Goldburn was good, but their soldiers had not been training for ruthless combat since they were children. Ko's men were highly skilled, well-armed, and tightly disciplined narco-terrorists. This particular team's hobbies for the past twenty years had been genocide of dissidents and murdering Chinese soldiers they captured from their outposts bordering the Shan State. He opened communications with the man they served, the mysterious Weng Lo Lew.

"Sir, we have fifty men on the estate, some are within yards of the house. I have the rest of the force ready to take down the military base. We can move on your command."

Ko and his forces were not part of the formal military supported by the false government of Myanmar used to placate the fools at the United Nations. They were Shan… a near lawless state of drug traffickers, human traffickers, and genocidal maniacs. They had wiped out all who have opposed them for over seven hundred years. Foreign intelligence agencies called their leader a War Lord, a silly western euphemism for a ruthless dictator of an international criminal powerhouse, feared by every legitimate government in the world, yet almost unknown to the rest of the planet's population.

The ex officio Shan State leader, Weng Lo Lew, spoke. "Leave them a message that will be unmistakably clear. I want the Chinese to experience misery and suffering. I want the subject of this mission to be humiliated and tortured. And then give the same courtesy to whatever force shows up first to investigate. Capture at least one alive for questioning. I don't think this will be our only task.

Our benefactors in the US government want this slowed down. They have been immensely helpful to us. Let's not let them down. The next mission might be even bigger."

"I don't think we will need everyone we brought for this assignment. How many men shall I use?" Ko asked.

"All of them."

Ko smiled. "It shall be done." He knew Weng Lo Lew's words meant a total massacre of every living thing in the area, and no one would ever know from where this act of terror came. Ko, a highly educated man, reflected on the power of their organization. *What was it that the American Quaker Wilkerson said? Ah, yes. One artifice of Satan is to induce men to believe that he does not exist.*

## MANILA, PHILIPPINES

The hot tub was on a secluded private balcony overlooking the bay. Pearson took a sip of his mojito as he soaked. Having a suite in an exclusive resort was one of the perks of working for a billionaire. "Mac… grab me another bowl of that chicken adobo."

Mac walked onto the balcony with two more cocktails. He set them down on the ledge of the tub and then went back in to get more food and some iced-down beer. When he returned, he hopped in the big tub and guzzled some of his drink. "This is living, Mr. Pearson. I'm glad we had a couple of days off before the next operation."

"About that… These bullet holes could really use more time to heal before the next little party, Mac. But I got to power through it for this New Zealand gig. Truth is, I'm not as young as I used to be."

Mac shrugged and pulled a San Miguel out of the ice bucket. *Nobody is as young as they used to be*, he thought. *Stupid comment to make. Especially for an immortal bastard like Mister Pearson.*

Pearson continued, shifting from relaxed to grim. "Which brings me to the point."

"What point?"

"I'm not always going to be able to do this shit at optimal levels… someday, a very distant someday, I might have to turn this shop over to you, or maybe someone smart, I don't know... but for now, you. And you'll need a suitable back-up."

Mac was surprised by the comments. "Backup? Wait, what?"

"Yes… you'll need someone to cover your back. I have somebody in mind, but that person still needs to be cleared by the boss. He's a little sensitive about hiring lately."

"You'll never retire, Mr. Pearson."

"I most certainly *am* going to retire. Especially if you act like a dick about this."

"I'm not being a dick; I just figure you'll get killed before we can retire."

"We?"

"I'm not getting any younger either, sir."

"You're thirty-two years old, dumb shit. You got decades of service ahead of you. Whereas me, being older, smarter, and better than you, I have decades of hot tubs and super-models in my future."

"So then, will I be boss?" Mac asked.

"Never," the old man scolded.

"Yes, I will."

Pearson pushed back. "No… you won't… for two very good reasons."

"Oh yeah, what's that?" suspecting the old man didn't have two reasons.

"One… you are an asshole…"

Mac shrugged, acknowledging that reason was probably legitimate. "Yeah, so…"

"And two, you are an asshole," Pearson said in a very self-satisfied way, wrapping his reasoning up like a good defense attorney delivering an effective closing argument.

Mac protested. "You just repeated one reason."

The old man shook his finger in Mac's face "It bore repeating."

"Grouchy old fart."

"Asshole."

They both resumed drinking beer.

Mac inquired casually, "So, who *is* this new backup person?"

Pearson remained elusive about the topic. "Never mind. You'll know when I think you need to know."

Mac pried, "Military?"

"Of course."

"What branch."

"Marine."

"I thought you despised jar heads." Mac was genuinely surprised.

"I don't despise them. I just prefer people who aren't jar heads… like Rangers."

"So why the switch?" Now Mac was genuinely curious.

"I found someone specifically skilled for this kind of work and I'm not an asshole."

"Interesting."

"You don't have to worry about it. What you need to worry about is us heading for New Zealand tomorrow to whack that next dipshit from that dipshit tech company full of dipshits."

Mac feigned fear, "Oh no, we're fighting dipshits?"

"Afraid so. Heavily fortified and well protected dipshits. This will not be a tropical vacation like Hawaii. This will be serious."

"How serious?"

"Oh, average."

---

## LAKE TEKAPO - SOUTH ISLAND, NEW ZEALAND ESTATE

*Hiding is the brave thing to do…* Gary Graham Goldburn, the billionaire CEO of Brazilo kept telling himself that… he was a very competent liar, even when lying to himself. He'd suffered not-stop diarrhea and the shakes since he got word about the untimely deaths of Featherston, Winger, and that little whiny sack of shit Shumway. Two in LA and One on Hawaii… *but are the killers heading west across the Pacific? That is the big question.* He barked at his head of security. "For heaven's sake, don't stand there. Do something!"

"You're perfectly safe here, sir," the hulking goon explained for the tenth time. "There is no way they are coming all the way to New Zealand. And if they do, we're more than ready."

Goldburn squirmed. "Bullshit... these guys are US military... or cops... or military cops.... You know, bad people. They're all Nazis and fascists and racists and sexists... they're terrible... and I know they are coming to uh... *get me*. It's your job to make sure they don't *get me*... not blather out pointless platitudes about being safe... They're killers... and they will kill me if you don't stop them. For what I pay for security, I'd think you'd appreciate that more."

The security operator pondered his situation, *I wonder what the consequences of shooting this spineless puss instead of protecting him... but a job is a job.* He tried giving an answer that might make his boss stop talking to him. "Sir, we have our men, the Chinese special forces, and the mercenary contractors covering the grounds. We are thousands of miles from them. Nobody is going to *get you*."

As the security man spoke, Goldburn's boyfriend unsteadily wandered out from the bedroom wearing only a gold mesh Speedo and a gaudy purple straw cowboy hat while noisily sipping, or more accurately slurping, champagne... "Darling, please listen to these nice men... I'm sure they know what they're doing." He made eyes at the security chief who blandly smiled and ignored him.

Standing at about five-foot-seven and, if soaking wet, weighing in at one-hundred-and-thirty-four pounds, Bilson Butterbottom was not rallying much confidence in the quality of the estate security with his drunken blathering. Butterbottom, formerly a coffee shop barista known as Bilson Werner, had been enjoying the good life as Goldburn's secret live-in boyfriend for over two years and carried more weight in the organization than his contributions merited.

Goldburn continued whining, "Stop it, Bilson…" he stomped his foot. "Stop it this very minute. We have terribly bad men coming here. Trained killers who kill people because of their training… and these horrible men want to kill us."

"Kill *you*," Bilson corrected, wondering how his benefactor ever survived grade school. Bilson resumed strutting around the room mentally contemplating the manliness of his current paramour, *I'm simply flaming and I'm less of a puss than this knob… Thank goodness he's rich.*

Goldburn barked back. "Kill *me*? Do you think they won't slaughter *all* of us? They're all deplorables… redneck hillbillies… Who do you think joins the military? They have no regard for the *better* people. I'm absolutely certain they will dispatch hundreds of commandos from… wherever they keep commandos… This is awful."

The head security somehow found the inner strength to resist the urge to barf but decided to get out of there anyway. "I'm going to check the perimeter, sir. Please remain here until I can return." His words and demeanor didn't reveal his actual thoughts, which were, *I need to take a Goldburn and wipe my Bilson.*

## THE TOWER RESORT HOTEL - CENTURY CITY – MANILA, PHILIPPINES

Mac heard the knock on the door and walked across the three-thousand square foot suite from the balcony to the entrance.

"Who is it?"

"Deeter," the President's son said, using his code name, which he thought was cool.

"Who is it?" Pearson yelled from his room.

"Deeter," Mac yelled back.

"Well let his ass in," Pearson shouted from his room.

Mac undid the locks and opened the door. Deeter had an armful of documents, maps, digital tablets, and a package wrapped in plain brown paper and sealed with heavy tape. Mac helped him carry his burden and placed the items on the dining room table.

Mr. Pearson emerged from his bedroom. "So, Deeter… what brings you to the beautiful Philippines?"

"Intelligence files and more operating funds." Deeter pulled a folding knife from his belt, flicked it open with one hand, and opened the package. It contained tightly wrapped bundles of hundred-dollar bills.

"Call the President of the Philippines if you have need of any additional equipment. He's a good guy. No limits… just get what you need and take this turd out." Deeter handed Pearson a business card with the Filipino President's private cell number. "He will provide you anything up to and including tanks, bombers, and boats."

Pearson accepted the business card with a wolfish smile. "That sounds like a plan."

"Nice," Mac mumbled, not sure what to say when someone drops off a half-million-dollar care package.

"You might need it. It seems like you are getting into some deep shit with this assignment and we've found that there are elements in Washington DC who are actively out to stop you."

"*Very* nice," Mac mumbled again only this time with a heavy dose of sarcasm. He imagined rogue CIA and FBI personnel hunting him and Pearson down like animals… which wouldn't be a big problem, but who has time to deal with that?

The Commander in Chief's son continued. "So, one other thing. The President says you are also clear to add another operative to the team if you wish."

Pearson frowned. "Do we no longer have his confidence?"

"Without a doubt, you have his confidence. You have the total confidence of the entire organization. But you also have a major force made up of some of the worst dregs in the mercenary world securing the perimeter of the target and running random patrols, Chinese covert military assholes, random miscellaneous assholes, and the entire elite security team of the next target waiting to kill you the moment you get close to New Zealand."

Mac wasn't comfortable with crowds, and the number three is widely known as the number that constitutes a crowd. "Oh… well, okay… but we've always been a two-man team… Who is this third guy?" he asked suspiciously.

Deeter put a hand up to slow down the process. "It doesn't matter who it is. It's up to Mr. Pearson if he chooses to add another member. Let's not get ahead of ourselves."

Pearson played it by the numbers, "Deeter is correct. Let's not get ahead of ourselves. First, let's look over the intelligence. What do you have, son?"

Deeter quickly set up the digital tablet and laid out the papers in a way that would make the intelligence presentation more fluid. "You will be going to the area of Lake Tekapo on the southern island of New Zealand. The target has a massive estate in the hills above the town. There is a military base nearby."

"Good," Mac and Pearson both said at the same time.

"No... bad. He used his influence with the New Zealand government to have it closed. He bought the abandoned base for a small fee and a big bribe. Now one of his holding companies leases it to China for special forces military training."

"I thought the current government in New Zealand was against guns and military stuff," Mac said.

"I'm afraid not... not if the price is right. Their commie leaders love guns in the hands of sympathetic extremist groups and foreign government organizations. Especially if the turds they allow to be armed can make these nitwit government officials feel enlightened and virtuous."

"That sounds about right," Pearson mumbled.

"So here we have it..." He passed his hand over the map. "A small town with a constable on the Brazilo corporate payroll. There's a seaport nearby, Timaru. Let me clarify, not exactly nearby but an hour-and-a-half drive." He pointed to another spot. "Here is the military base. That's where the

Chinese live. There is usually seventy-five in training and twenty-five on duty at the estate at any given time. We estimate one hundred other random mercenaries securing the outer perimeter and patrolling... not great troops but just okay... still, they always assign at least thirty of their men to be active on the estate grounds protecting the asset.

He put away the map and directed attention to an intelligence report put together by a mysterious foundation referred to vaguely as *Friends of the United States*. The report had no formal headings, names, or abstracts. It was a long narrative with lots of bullet points and spread sheets. It also included a map marked up in tactical grids highlighting enemy forces, potential defensive positions, and possible exfiltration plans.

"There is an on-site security force made up of top-notch elite international mercenaries, war contractors, and former foreign fighters as we call them, from the Middle East. We don't have an exact number, but I'm going to guess that there is at least one hundred of those assholes."

"Shit." Pearson rubbed his wounded shoulder. "It will take an entire day to kill all these shit birds."

"It gets even worse. The house is on the side of a hill. It's heavily fortified. They own the high ground if things go south. The windows are bulletproofed, and the doors are reinforced steel, on steel frames with heavy duty steel hinges."

"Can't we just nuke it from space?"

"Sure, but that leaves evidence and requires too many bodies involved to keep it secret. Don't forget, this will put us only about halfway through the project."

Mac looked at Pearson, who was carefully going through the paperwork. Mac thought he looked more pissed off than usual and he was favoring his shoulder in a big way. Taking a round through the meaty part of the shoulder takes longer than a day or so to heal, even for Pearson.

Deeter asked, "So what about adding bodies to our team?"

Pearson issued a pregnant thousand-yard stare to Deeter and then slowly turned to dose Mac with stink eye. His grizzled face said, I *should kill everyone in the room*, but a few guttural words escaped the scarred maw on his face that he called a mouth, "Not yet... I'm still alive and I told your father that I would take care of this. I gave my word. We will hit it in two days."

Mac thought he heard Deeter gulp... twice. *Some bridges are best uncrossed,* he thought. The old man gives his word... that's the end of a discussion. He's doing whatever it was he said he would do.

Deeter stumbled through an awkward okay and farewell, then left, leaving Mac and Pearson alone in the room.

## SOUTH ISLAND, NEW ZEALAND — TWO DAYS LATER

The sun was setting when a sea plane, flown by one of the President's personal pilots, got them close enough to get access the island with an inflatable boat. The ocean was like glass. Mac started the small gas-powered four-cycle engine with one pull and then piloted it to a remote shoreline half an hour after complete darkness enveloped the coast.

Mac and Pearson dragged the boat up off the gravely beach and into the tree line. They concealed it with brush.

They organized their gear and marched briskly over a series of rolling hills. A car had been left on a dirt road, an hour's walk inland. It was a cheap old local rust bucket, but it ran well enough to transport them further up the coast and then inland near the target location.

This thing might be a piece of shit, but it's certainly better than humping this shit in on foot," Mac said.

The old man nodded, "For once I can't argue with you."

Before daybreak Mac and the Pearson were setting up camp on the ridge above their target and initiated surveillance.

"It seems awfully quite down there... and dark." Pearson didn't like it.

"Something's wrong." Mac said the words based on an instinct rather than evidence. "Let's get a recon done before daybreak."

Something was wrong.

It didn't take long to find everyone dead. All of them. Mercs, soldiers, security, and the target himself.

"What the hell?" Mac stood slack jawed at the base of the tree, shocked at the level of destruction and bloodshed caused by someone who wasn't him.

"Son of a bitch!" Pearson was surprised as well. "That's Goldburn." He pointed at the body in the tree.

Mac pulled out a photo and confirmed it. He agreed, "yeah... it *was* Goldburn."

Mac provided cover as Pearson drew a knife. He cut the body down from the tree that was used to crucify the technology icon. His eyes had been burned out, apparently while he was still alive. A knife was still embedded in his crotch and a piece of rebar had been shoved up his ass. *Everything considered, this loser had a bad day*, Pearson thought.

"I think everyone here is dead… but… *we* didn't kill them." Mac said, just wanting to throw the observation out there.

"Duh." Pearson answered curtly.

Mac knew his statement made him sound like a dick, mainly because this was an unbelievably dangerous situation and being a dick was his '*go to*' move under pressure. "You're too old to say shit like *duh*. I should say that. Not you."

Pearson wasn't listening.

Pearson's voice revealed an unusual hint of urgency. "We need to get out of here. Now."

"Yeah…" Mac agreed, his head on a swivel watching for threats.

Then the triangulated machine gun fire started. Mac grimaced. Nobody likes to be on the receiving end of triangulated machine gun fire, no matter how great your sense of humor is. A shit day had just turned into a shittier day.

# Chapter 8 – Never piss off a Burmese with a gun

## LAKE TEKAPO - SOUTH ISLAND, NEW ZEALAND ESTATE

Mercilessly, lead poured down on them from the ridgeline like a torrential death storm. Rounds pelted the rocks with increasing intensity as more troops concentrated fire in support of the machine guns. But the perfectly executed ambush had one small and unanticipated flaw. Mac and the old man were hard to kill.

"Who are these pricks?" Mac shouted as they attempted to climb up their own assholes seeking cover.

"My guess is they are a bunch of assholes."

"Yeah, I agree. I can't say I'm a huge fan of them."

They hunkered down under a large rock outcropping. Pearson did a quit diagram in the soft soil with his finger.

"The bulk of the fire seems to be coming from two points. I think our best bet is to deploy a claymore facing the placement at the ridgeline…" He pointed on his dirt map. "Then we lay fire on placement two by the rocks here." The old man barked orders as he pointed to his best guess was for the second gun emplacement location.

Mac fished the claymore out of his ruck and waited for a lull in fire to place it. There wasn't one.

A voice pierced the gunfire… amplified… perhaps an electronic megaphone.

"Surrender or we engage the mortars."

"Mortars? Well fuck me to tears," the old man muttered, angry at himself for dropping his guard at the sight of the crucified tech giant. It was an error, perhaps even a fatal error, but there is no place for regret in a gunfight.

He did a quick peek around the edge of the rock. It looked like hundreds of soldiers were forming up around the ridgeline preparing for an assault. Not ideal. Megaphone man was standing in the middle, a scrawny ugly-assed bastard with a big X shaped scar on his head.

He turned back to his partner. "We're screwed, Mac. Crawl down that little ditch when I start shooting. I'll try to give you some cover. You might get out."

"Yeah, but no. I'll never make it and we both die anyway."

"Surrender doesn't work for me."

"We can't let them make us talk."

"Then we don't talk. Mission first, boy. Get this intelligence back to the boss. He needs to know what's coming. He has a treasonous rat on the inside and we got to stop them before these maggots make every son of a bitch on the planet their slave." He paused and then lied. "I'll be fine. I'll exfiltrate some other way. Leave me that bag of goodies you pulled that claymore out of."

Mac didn't like it. But there was no choice this time. Getting sacrificed was part of the job, but it's easier when it's you instead of somebody else… someone you might care about if you were the kind of person who cared. But the options were gone.

He unslung the canvas bag and placed it on the ground between them. Mac took a quick peek. He could see megaphone man on the ridgeline. He'd remember that prick.

## LAKE TEKAPO - SOUTH ISLAND, NEW ZEALAND - RIDGELINE

Ko might have had primitive roots but his master's in psychology from Brown University provided deep insight into the thought processes of the western warrior class. They would be prepared to die trying to report back to their leader. He smiled. That was exactly what he wanted them to do. One to keep for questioning and one to take a message back… it was time for the President to learn that there was more than one dog in this fight. Time for the upstart leader to learn his place.

*** 

In the rocks at the edge of the estate grounds, Mac pulled of his glove and offered his hand to Pearson.

Pearson shared an uncharacteristic smile and pulled off his glove.

They shook hands.

"Do what's right, kid. I'm in my happy place. It's all good." Pearson thought he saw some moisture in Mac's right eye… and his left eye. Shit. He felt wetness in his own eyes.

Mac gathered himself and replied. "Thank you, sir. I'll do my best to honor you with my life."

The old man started to say something… then didn't. He just nodded his head… it was time to suck it up and kick ass for America. He took a deep breath, grinned for the first time in Mac's memory, and winked. "Get to work, you pussy. I got assholes to kill."

Mac spared the old man any more emo bullshit. He turned, scrambled down in the small ditch and disappeared into the brush. There was a job to be done… come hell or high water.

On the ridgeline above, Ko gave the order to advance and capture a prisoner and to allow one to escape. Two hundred highly skilled terrorist commandos moved out from cover to execute the order.

## WASHINGTON D.C.

The President called his two most trusted advisors into his private office. His son and daughter took chairs across from his desk, like they had done so many times before in their lives.

"I believe our two *friends* are in trouble. It appears as if a very high-ranking intelligence official might have taken steps to undermine their mission and set a trap."

His son spoke first. "We already know they want to destroy the United States and turn us into a socialist shit hole. Which one though?"

The daughter, always the most insightful asked a salient question in the fashion of the Spartans. "One?"

The President smiled. "Exactly. There are dozens of these infestations in our intelligence agencies. The Russians, the Chinese, the Iranians, all our enemies have made incredible inroads into infiltrating our government. But I'll be very straightforward here… I'm not sure these traitors are fully aware of the extent of our enemies' intent. I can't believe anyone born in this amazing and beautiful country would do that."

Deeter thought about that for a moment before replying. "Dad... Mr. President. I don't mean to dispute your opinion but… I think a lot of them have willingly sold out. The more we dig, the worse it gets."

His daughter added, "He's right. I think the only ones we can trust are in this room and your two uh… specialists. And of course, the Vice-President."

"I agree. I can handle these opportunistic elected officials. They are a clown show. They wouldn't last a second in real estate, that I can tell you. I can even manage most of the deep state and the press. I have patriotic friends helping who you are not, and never will be, aware of. But nevertheless, I must be cautious moving forward and the… what did you call them? Oh yeah, specialists… they are the key to protecting our citizens, our country, and western civilization… truly the last line of defense for the Republic."

The siblings nodded in agreement.

The President continued. "I'm adding another. Mr. Pearson gave me a folder. I need you both to take a long and detailed look at it. This person's history is highly classified. After your review we'll decide on whether to bring this person on board. Mr. Pearson's recommendation carries a lot of weight with me. But I need your review. I think we need a third person to support their activity despite his inclination to keep it to two.

The president handed a printed folder to each of them. He was old school and didn't trust computers although he exploited technology to manipulate and aggravate his opponents at every opportunity.

The two advisors left the room to study the contents of the folders.

## LAKE TEKAPO - SOUTH ISLAND, NEW ZEALAND — RIDGELINE

There was a lull in fire as Ko's men advanced. Pearson pulled a Cohiba out of his pocket and lit the stubby cigar. It was time to go to work.

He rolled partially out of his position of cover and assumed a prone position. Lining up his sights, he pressed the trigger and fired.

A terrorist slumped to the ground.

The old man repeated the process five more times. The advancing force did not slow down.

He rolled to the other side of the rocks. He estimated range at seventy-five yards… it looked like a mass charge was in the works. Outstanding.

Pearson dug into Mac's goody bag and dug out another claymore mine. Perfect. Two should do the job. He placed one on each side of his hidey hole. This side towards enemy was probably his favorite thing to read on a weapon. For some reason it always warmed his heart to see it.

Next he dug out four fragmentation grenades. He jammed them into his pockets. The last item was a Mac Special. A nylon bag full of 16D common framing nails, buckshot, and short bits of barbed wire with a quarter pound of C4 and a detonator. In fact, Deeter had stocked all their secret armories around the world with the custom explosive packages. Pearson used a carabiner attached to the bag and clipped the bomb onto the back of his belt.

He topped off the 1911 and M4…

Pearson couldn't remember the last time he had this much fun. His worst fear was getting too old to operate, sitting in a nursing home unable to wipe his own ass, stuck in a room with a bunch of other geezers watching the View and unable to put a well-placed round through the boob tube… Advance directly to hell, do not pass go, do not collect two hundred dollars sounded much better than that crock of a disgusting-assed future. This was his lucky day.

Checking out on his own terms after a life of adventure and balls out fun, surrounded by stacks of dead enemies. It was like winning the lottery.

Quick peek. Forty yards… thirty more seconds and the show could start.

\*\*\*

Ko watched as his men converged on the rocky ledge where the commando was hiding. He smiled… the lone American was probably shitting his pants. Without drones, technology, and overwhelming force, the Americans were weak and pathetic. He picked up the electronic megaphone and gave the order… Attack!

\*\*\*

Pearson heard the command. He knew what it meant. He snorted a laugh, counted to five, and fired the first claymore. He peeked around the rocks and enjoyed the splash of red that swept up the rocks and the screams of maimed men dying slow horrible deaths.

"I bet you pricks felt that shit," He yelled. "Here's some more, you bastards!"

He fired the second claymore. More death screams. More crimson blood. More body parts flying through the air like party poppers. Good times.

*Murdering assholes is so relaxing,* he thought.

Pearson took a long puff on the Cohiba, readied himself, and then peeled out at a low run on the port side of the rocks, and charged uphill. *You want to see an attack you commie asshole? I'll grant that fucking wish.*

At least thirty or forty dead out of the two hundred or so dirt bags, he estimated as he surveyed his field of battle. Most of the claymore survivors were just emerging from cover after the blasts. Pearson fired at anything that moved.

An enemy combatant stood up to take aim at him. He fired first hitting the man in the face. Three others appeared to starboard. A short burst from the M4 took them down. So far, so good.

Further up the hill a man lined up his AK47 and fired a short burst of 7.62X39 rounds.

One hit. Pearson stumbled... got up... ran ahead. A flesh wound across the side. No biggie.

Pearson countered and popped the man with a three-round burst... all center mass... red spots on his chest... the shooter dropped, disappearing into the low scrub brush.

Five more closed, firing, running. The old man went prone, fired an aimed round at each of them. Five down. He hopped up and sprinted at a slight diagonal to the remaining forces.

He felt a hand grasp at his ankle. A wounded guy he thought was dead tripped him, causing him to drop his rifle. He pulled his 45 as he fell and shot that grabby-assed maggot in the eye.

More men coming… he picked up his M4 and emptied the magazine on fully automatic fire forcing them to drop and take cover. A couple dropped because they were dead too.

*Ha!*

This time the old man stayed low. Too many of them converging. Crawling he moved through the wounded and dying. He found a small ditch and reloaded the rifle. He pulled a grenade out of his pocket, jerked out the pin and tossed it.

A small group of the enemy went down.

*Sweet.*

He followed up with single aimed shots at scrambling targets. Six more down. Roll to port and find some more cover… moving… a boulder gave some respite.

*Shit.*

He realized he'd been hit three more times. He hadn't noticed at first. Nothing bad but not really great either. Flesh wounds.

*Keep moving.*

Toss another grenade. Wait five seconds. Toss another grenade.

*How do you like that shit?*

Some of the assholes were falling back… scrambling back up the steep sloping hill. Pussies.

Take aim… Fire. Repeat.

He began crawling again… this time straight up. He found two dead guys sort of stacked. Perfect cover. He adjusted the bodies a bit to provide a better firing position. He began delivering sustained fire and got into a rhythm. Fire. Fire. Fire. Throw a grenade. Pearson smiled. This was going perfectly.

*Shit.*

A rifle round clocked his shoulder… a solid hit. Left side… Damn it. Some bastard got behind him… probably another dickhead playing possum. Pearson pulled the 45 out with his right hand and took aim. Fire… Fire.

A counterattack was forming higher up… then the swarm came… a bayonet charge.

*This is bullshit!*

He did a one handed reload of the 45… it was awkward but worked. *You think you're gonna overrun my ass? Like hell*, he thought. He managed to get to his feet and charged them.

The change of dynamic confused the attackers enough to slow their momentum. Instinctively they parted to the sides of the old man's path.

Pearson raised his 45 with his good arm and started popping off assholes of opportunity. He emptied his gun and pulled his KaBar knife. They were on him. The first bayonet speared his leg. He started to go down but not before returning the favor and stabbing an enemy in the femoral artery. He felt the warm blood spray covering his face… *Perfect,* he thought… *dying in battle, drenched in the blood of my enemies. It doesn't get better than this.*

Forty of the surviving attackers scrambled down from cover and crowded in to watch the final kill.

Pearson bellowed a defiant death scream and pulled the pin on the explosive pack dangling off the back of his belt. He fell on his back, speared by bayonets at least a dozen times.

He growled his final words, *"Fuck you, assholes!"*

Three seconds later the explosion rocked the sloping hillside.

The explosion caused the grenades and rounds the enemy carried to cook off in a burst of fire, guts, and brains as the force of the blast carried every piece of metal on their bodies out another hundred yards as shrapnel, shredding the pack of them into ground raw meat.

Blood ran down the hillside like flood water raging through a dry desert wash following a torrential thunderstorm. Hell had come to earth, and it wasn't pretty.

Then it was quiet.

Ko picked himself up off the ground after the blast. He was painted from head to foot with the blood and guts of his dead men. He was the last man alive on the hill. All his troops were dead or dying.

He pulled a silk handkerchief from his pocket and wiped the gore from his eyes. Ko was impressed. He paid final tribute to his target.

"Damn… *That* was a man."

\*\*\*

Mac looked over his should as the last bomb detonated. He knew what that meant. He understood the nature of the old man's sacrifice. But soon it would be time for revenge. He thought about going back and finishing the job, but he knew it wasn't the right time. Payback would come soon enough. He tried to freeze frame the face of the enemy force's leader in his mind. Asian, lean, with a distinctive scar on his forehead above his right eye that looked like an X. That son of bitch, if still alive, was going to pay for this shit.

Mac got into the RIB boat, headed to sea, and called for pick up… *Pearson's gone… I can't believe Pearson's gone.*

# Chapter 9 – Never piss off a Marine with a gun

## THE GREAT HALL OF THE PEOPLE - BEIJING

Zhao stared down the men seated at the conference table with him. His face barely concealed his rage. "Who killed our men? Who killed Goldburn? What the hell happened?

The man to his immediate right squirmed a bit in his chair and began to speak. "We believe it was…"

The report of the pistol startled everyone in the room as the man flopped back in his seat revealing a round black hole above his right eyebrow.

The minister of agriculture sitting next to the body shit himself. It was going to be another one of those kinds of meetings.

Zhao slowly raised the gun barrel to his lips and blew away the smoke. He didn't even look at the dead man sitting next to him. "You are all replaceable, like this one." He gestured with the gun at their deceased comrade with the smoking hole in his forehead. "I want full reports on my desk in four hours. I want surveillance photos. I want to know who is behind this. If you do not know and have nothing to contribute, you can sign out a weapon and end your pathetic lives. Meeting adjourned."

## NEW YORK CITY – CNT WORLD NEWS BROADCASTING

Jennifer Calbado felt she was on to something. She didn't know what it was, but she was going to make it sound as terrible as possible at the President's expense.

"Investigators are trying to determine why flags are at half-staff at every property the President owns world-wide. Is this some kind of new Alt-Right conspiracy? A dog-whistle perhaps, sent to alert his most extremist followers? Or is it a signal for something else? The White House has been suspiciously quiet about it. We will continue to report and investigate."

The director indicated the shot was complete and the teleprompter flickered off.

Calbado turned to her assistant who was desperately applying makeup to her face. "Do you think we nailed that prick? I know it must be Hitler's birthday or something. Get out there and find out why he did this. He is such a Nazi."

"Yes, ma'am." The assistant replied trying to tune out her horrible news-bitch boss.

"And bring me a latte and a salad… something with protein, no gluten, and Italian dressing… and a shredded beef burrito… and a hamburger. I'm vegan but I have a condition that requires additional carbs and stuff."

"Yes ma'am." The young woman quickly scribbled the order on her ubiquitous mole notebook

The director signaled that it was time to shoot the next scene. He cued Jennifer and the cameras went live.

"In our next report… the President's diet. Why is he so unhealthy and fat?"

## THE TOWER RESORT HOTEL - CENTURY CITY – MANILA, PHILIPPINES

On the balcony of the hotel, Mac stretched out on a chair with a bottle of Jack Daniels in his hand experiencing a little introspection.

"I don't even know if I still have a job. The only person I ever got close to is dead. And the mission isn't completed. Life sucks."

Saying it aloud didn't induce a flurry of new epiphanies. His words were tantamount to a pathetic whine and he knew it. But today he felt pathetic.

The lifestyle of his job precluded having friends, at least people who might find themselves close enough to him to figure out what he did for a living. It was a lonely life.

His cell phone rang. It was Deeter.

"Mac, I'm so sorry," the President's son offered his words of condolence. "Pearson was a great man. Are you doing okay?"

"Never better."

"Seriously?"

"I'm fine. Do I still have a job?"

"Of course. Mr. Pearson expressed very clearly that if something like this happened, you were ready to take charge. He had total confidence in you."

Mac felt his eyes well up... must be allergies.

Deeter continued, "Might I come and discuss this with you?"

"Sure, boss. I'll be here."

"I'll be there at one in the afternoon tomorrow your time.

The call disconnected.

Mac felt his chin trembling. *Dammit*... It was too late to try to control it. He didn't want to control it, he hadn't the strength to hold it back anymore. He started bawling, weeping, and sobbing without restraint. The dam of emotion crumbled. He couldn't stop. All the smack talk and macho bullshit melted away as he was slapped across the face with the reality that he lost someone he loved like a father and would never see that old man again.

## THE TOWER RESORT HOTEL - HONOLULU

Deeter called his father on the secure phone. He picked up on the first ring.

"Son, are you doing okay?"

"Sure, dad… It's a sad day for all of us… for America… but we must persevere. No one else is going to step up."

"That's the spirit. Pearson was a great man. Some day when I'm gone, I'd love it if you would author a book about him. Tell the true story of what's happening to our country and how a brave man tried to stop it at the cost of his life."

Deeter nodded although he was alone. "Consider it done. But what do we do now? The threat is still viable."

"Get Mac some back-up first thing. That will get us operational again. It might seem cold to keep moving forward so soon after losing Pearson, but business is business, and this is the country's business. If he could tell us so, Pearson would agree. Our primary job will be to figure out who else is out there. Who wiped out the New Zealand operation? Then we need the location of the facility where the bioweapon is being built. I don't think I can trust its destruction to anyone outside our core group. I need to know the identity of the asshole who killed Pearson, and have Mac kill that dirt bag. He's a horrible, horrible person. Purely evil."

"Check." Deeter wrote as he listened.

The President continued delivering rapid fire direction, "And we need to re-engage the remaining conspirators and finish the job. We need to take all of these bastards out of the gene pool."

"So, I call the candidate?"

"Yes… the candidate is vacationing in Thailand… if you call knife fighting a vacation." The President laughed.

Deeter could almost see his facial expressions and could visualize how he turns his head when he jokes about something.

The President added more direction. "Call her but tell Mac first before they meet. Break it to him face to face. Then we will have her come in.

"Copy that."

"Good luck, son… and thank you."

## TOWER RESORT HOTEL – MANILA, PHILIPPINES

Deeter took a sip of iced tea before speaking. "It was the old man's wish that we assign a new partner to you in the event of his death. He even selected someone for the job."

Deeter explained the situation to Mac over a room service lunch on the balcony of Mac's hotel room overlooking downtown Manila. "We've completed all the background checks and personal history research. An amazing person really."

Mac shoved a chunk of spicy chicken breast into his mouth. "I understand. I'll need to meet him, and we'll need some time for training."

Deeter took a last bite of salad and pushed the plate away. The discussion went more smoothly than he had hoped. "Fine. I'll notify the candidate immediately. She is in Bangkok this week teaching a bladed weapons class to their elite military forces." Deeter didn't tell him that she was in an illegal knife fighting competition and perhaps some of their elite military forces were competitors… training sounded more… reasonable.

"Whoa!" Mac was confused… "Did you say *she*?"

Deeter put a hand up like a traffic cop. "Mac. It's Erica Falcone… I believe you know who she is."

"The woman?"

Deeter gave him an odd look. "Yes... She's a woman."

"The woman knife fighter?" Mac pressed.

"I believe that's how she is known in some circles," Deeter replied. "thus, the exposition in Thailand right now."

Mac stood up. "She's crazy... and besides, I heard the Marines discharged her for getting blown up or something."

Deeter pressed. "One... in this situation, Dad insists that we might need crazy... it's almost a job requirement. Two, she didn't get hurt *that* bad. It was just a punctured lung, some shrapnel, and a massive concussion."

"Just?"

Deeter added, "And some other shit... like some bullet holes."

"Then why did they let her go?" Mac wasn't buying it. A jarhead, a woman, a woman who had already been blown up... not good, he thought. The human body can only get blown up so many times and in this job, getting blown up was as routine as running out of printer paper at a normal business.

Deeter answered, "Deniability issues... Something about a nuclear explosion across the border in Mexico, three hundred dead cartel members in Arizona, and you know…" his voice trailed off.

"Know what?"

"Eagle Rock."

"No shit?" McCartney said incredulously.

"Forget I mentioned it," Deeter added.

"Forgotten, dude… I prefer living." Mac scratched his head. "She's definitely qualified. Half that bullshit going around about Eagle Rock sounds like crap out of a Bronco Hammer book."

Deeter nodded. "America's greatest literary genius."

Mac was on board. "How soon can she join us? And is she okay with suicide missions?"

Deeter elaborated, "She prefers suicide missions… regular missions are too… what was that she called them? Too pussified." He paused and thought a second before continuing. "I'm not sure that's a real word… but I think we all know what she meant. With Dad ending all these US foreign adventures, there isn't much left in the Middle East to keep her interested anymore."

"And again, how soon?"

"Tomorrow morning. You'll have another day of recovery and then you'll have two days to prepare for the invasion."

"Invasion? Strong term. I like it."

## Ninoy Aquino International Airport – Manila, Phillippines

"So, you *have* met her?" Mac asked the President's son as they sat in the vehicle.

"A few times… some low-key interviews… a couple of phone calls."

"And no one told me because…"

"Exactly."

"Oh…"

A woman exited the terminal… she was breathtakingly beautiful… long dark hair, lean, yet muscular in a sexy way… She didn't look like a dangerous operator. She looked like a model for some health and fitness company, except she had big boobs. Her attire was simple… tan shorts, a pink tank top, pink ball cap, and pink flip-flops. What made her stand out was the sixty pounds of black rucksack hoisted over her shoulder. She strode up to the duo's vehicle. She leaned into the window and eyeballed Mac. "Hey Junior, what the hell is this turd supposed to be, your dog pound rescue?"

Deeter almost smiled. "No… meet McCartney… you can call him Mac or asshole… he answers to both."

"Hi, Asshole. Secure this ruck for me. I have to go back to customs and pick up my weapons." She dropped her bag and started to turn back towards the terminal.

Mac yelled back. "Nice to meet you, jarhead. Why don't you kiss my hairy ass?"

She paused, turned, and made a fake pouty face. "Did I forget to say please, little man?"

Mac kept his eyes forward, avoiding the temptation to steal a glimpse at her cleavage. "Yes, you did. Not that I'd carry your shit for you anyway. We carry our own weight around here."

She shrugged. "Fair enough." Falcone stepped back and cleared her throat before starting over. "Mac, will you please secure this shit while I get the rest of my other shit?"

He smiled. "I'd be happy to."

They flipped each other off. Then Mac exited the vehicle and placed the duffel in the back. Falcone disappeared back into the airport.

Mac stuck his head in the window and addressed Deeter. "She seems nice."

"She's your kind of people, Mac. You can trust her."

"We'll see," Mac responded, remaining skeptical.

Deeter was growing frustrated with Mac's concerns. "You'll see in the next day or so. Just do what needs to be done. She'll be fine."

"I know, it just seems like women are always bad luck… it has a lot to do with them being women."

"I hear you, Mac… just give her a chance."

"I will… if that psycho hottie doesn't murder me in my sleep."

"Could you blame her?"

Mac gave that response some thought. "No… I can't say that I could."

## LANGLEY, VIRGINIA

Clammer wiped sweat of his brow with a cheap cotton handkerchief even though the air conditioner was on. He felt like he might either vomit, have diarrhea, or both. How did this thing get so messed up? Bodies strewn all over New Zealand, crucified tech giants, unknown mercenaries… what the hell was that maniac in Myanmar thinking?

The bright red desk phone rang. His secretary.

"Sir, the representative of the senior senator from New York is here for your meeting."

"What meeting?"

"Sir, I'm not sure. It was on my books when I got here this morning. Private meeting. Security has cleared your visitor."

"Send him in." Anything to take his mind off his irritable bowel. Even a meeting with some self-important senatorial staff puke might help.

Director Clammer looked up in surprise to see an attractive Asian woman standing before him. She stared at him with an odd smile, not speaking.

"Can I help you?" he asked.

She remained silent, motionless… as if she was waiting for something."

Clammer regained some of his normal bluster. "Excuse me, but who the hell are you supposed to be?"

She slowly approached him, moving deliberately, like a jungle feline. With blinding speed, she slid across the top of his desk, snatched his tie, and yanked him out of his chair. He fell on the floor, rolled involuntarily onto his back, and felt her on top of him. She had a knife. The point was in his ear. She leaned in close. He could smell her breath.

Clammer whimpered as she silently stared into his eyes like an optometrist examining a patient for glaucoma. The silence frightened him. *Shouldn't she ask me something? Anything*? Is she just going to murder me without speaking?

Finally, she spoke again. "Zhao is not happy, motherfucker."

*Shit…* Clammer wondered… *she has an Alabama accent. What the hell?*

"Zhao? He sent *you*? How did you get in here?"

"We own you… therefore, we own this agency."

"Why you…" he groused in a half-hearted attempt at a menacing tone of voice.

The woman wasn't having it. She poked the knife into his ear a little. "Shut up, asshole."

He was confused. Her accent wasn't what he expected. She sounded more like a southern moonshiner than a foreign spy. "What the hell? You can't talk to me like that. Do you know who I am?"

The woman didn't seem to give a fuck who he was. She twisted the knife a little deeper into his ear causing him to make a squeak toy sound. "Zhao is unhappy. You were supposed to take care of things. Make sure his operatives were protected. I should kill you right here in your office, you filthy American scum. Did you think sending in a small army to kill your own hit team was going to fool us?"

Clammer went to his default lying mode. "Hit team? Army? I don't know… I…" He paused, switching to his counter-accusation mode. "Wait a minute. How do I *really* know Zhao sent you?"

The woman wasn't tolerating his nonsense. She let him feel the back of her hand across his left cheek with a brutal smack and moved the knife to his nuts.

He yipped like a puppy that just sensed its tail being squished under a rocking chair. "Okay… I'm sorry… I believe Zhao sent you… what does he want me to do?" Clammer unsuccessfully tried rubbing the sting off his face with the palm of his hand… his eyes watered up. He involuntarily ripped a loud fart. *Oh no… that might have been a shart*, he thought.

The woman clutched his throat and squeezed. "First, never fart like that again in my presence. Second, you *will* protect our remaining assets. If we find your fingerprints on anything that happened in New Zealand, you'll be murdered in your sleep. No negotiation, no excuses, just dead. And one other thing. Zhao wants you to focus on undermining your President's popularity… accuse him of something. Anything. We are in desperate trade negotiations… and you are doing nothing to help. We have planted enough phony Russian evidence and fake bimbo stories to keep you busy for years with phony accusations. Do *not* fail Zhao again." She jammed the knife a little deeper into the testicle zone causing him to involuntarily emit another mouse squeak from his mouth and blow another wet note on his butt horn.

Clammer pleaded, "That shit wasn't even me… I think it was the Director of the FBI. He's a dick… and a puss… and an asshole… It wasn't me. I won't fail."

"The FBI Director?" She asked.

"Yeah, he said something about mercenaries and a special operation overseas. He probably did it."

"We'll see. But for now, you take care of this thing with your President. He can't interfere with our operations. We've invested too much in fools like you to allow that to happen."

Clammer whined, "The President is rude. You've read him on twitter. It will be easy. I'll make sure he's *really* investigated. I have more guys I can put on it. You won't have to come back."

She grinned evilly, "Oh, it won't be *me* who comes back. If you let our leader down again, he will send Mr. Kang. You don't want to meet Mr. Kang. You might wind up as the victim of a terrible suicide. You know how that works in this town."

Clammer started getting motorboat farts now. *Not Kang,* he thought... *he's the devil incarnate. An evil man of cruelty and unspeakable violence.* Clammer capitulated, "Fine... I'm on it," he said, resignation heavy in his voice. *I'm dead*, he thought.

She looked at him with disgust. "You stink like shit."

Clammer saw her fist draw back and then everything went blank... when he awoke, she was gone, he had a massive headache, and he needed to change his shorts. *That could have gone worse. At least it wasn't Kang*, he thought as he tried to roll over and get up.

## THE TOWER RESORT — MANILLA, PHILIPPINES

Deeter dropped the two specialists off at the bell captain stand and then directed his driver take him back to the airport.

As they entered the resort, Mac attempted some small talk. "We have a job to do, and by that, I mean I have a job to do. I'm not sure you're going to work out. Nobody told me about you."

"Yes, they did."

"No, they didn't."

"Pearson told me he told you."

Mac decided this debate wasn't going well and abandoned the tactic. "That doesn't matter."

Falcone threw a lifeline in an attempt to generate some positive communication between them. "What do you want to know?"

Mac asked bluntly, "What good are you?"

She considered the question a moment before answering. "I'm going to my suite, taking a bath, then in an hour, I'm going to go get a beer. You can meet me in the bar if you want and we can figure out what we're going to do."

Mac frowned. "What the hell does that mean?"

"It means kiss my ass. We have communists to kill. I don't have time for your weepy-assed horseshit.

172

I know your friend got killed. I met him and respected him. But lot of my friends get killed. It happens. You carry on."

Mac let that chunk of actual wisdom sink in a moment before answering. "Oh yeah." *When she's right, she's right,* he thought.

Falcone repeated her plan. "Yeah... meet me at the bar in an hour and we'll plan the next mission."

"Fine... but if you see an Asian dude with an X carved in his forehead, he's mine."

"Ko?"

"Huh?"

"Ko... Burmese asshole. Slender, mean looking..."

"You know him?"

"Who do you think carved that X on his forehead?" She winked.

Mac considered her words... *impressive*. No wonder the old man selected this warrior. That was some bad ass shit to say. He decided that perhaps he liked this woman after all. He'd give her a chance. "In an hour, we're meeting at the bar and getting a beer. Then we can plan the mission. That's an order."

"Copy that, kitty cat." She said with a vicious grin. She gave Mac the finger again and walked to her room.

Mac watched her leave. *She might work out okay.*

# Chapter 10 – Never piss off a mercenary with a gun

## WHITE HOUSE - WASHINGTON DC

The President and two of his children sat down in his private dining room with diet soft drinks and coffees.

The President vented, "These politicians are driving me nuts. They lie, blackmail, cheat, steal… it makes the New York construction business seem like a vacation at the Vatican. I'm totally serious."

"Dad, we knew that going in. What we didn't know is that we'd have more to worry about from the bureaucracy than from the elected ones," his daughter responded, always quick to provide a calming balance to her dynamic father.

Deeter added, "We need to decide how to handle the traitors. Should we '*direct action*' them with the specialists? I'm not sure we have a choice."

The President considered it, "Not at this time. I'll deal with them politically for now. We must save civilization first… then we'll see. If Mac finds out that they were behind the death of Pearson, we probably won't be consulted anyway. They signed their own death warrants when they crossed a man of violence."

"A man of violence?" his daughter asked hesitantly. She could see the grim determination in his eyes. He was about to say words a man doesn't wish to ever speak in front of his children, but a world was at stake, and they were ready… ready to hear the ugly side of the world at a level of which they knew nothing, in spite of their travels, education, and business experience.

He took a deep breath and slowly exhaled before continuing. "A man of violence is a person who is capable of things too terrible for decent people to discuss or even think about. He's capable of being a monster, although normal people don't recognize him as he walks among them. Somehow, they seem to recognize each other though."

He paused and took a sip of his beverage, then continued, "A man of violence has the potential for committing terrible acts of horror and seeing acts of horror day after day… his capacity for coping with the nightmare underbelly of the world, a place we would call hell, can only be described as immeasurable… he likes it there. Yet he isn't always what one would expect. A man of violence can be good or he can be evil… And despite all that, sometimes a man of violence is all we have with which to protect ourselves from the chaos… what Nietzsche referred to as the abyss. If a normal man, even a brave man, gazes for long into an abyss, the abyss gazes also into him. A man of violence peers into the abyss… and the abyss retreats to the darkness in stark terror, seeking safety in its own deepest shadows, forever shuddering in puddles of ice-cold rabid fear. The abyss fears him. Sometimes these men are cops, sometimes they are soldiers, and sometimes they are just bad mother fuckers who operate in the night never knowing a master and never knowing obedience to authority of any kind. It's best for us to let this go for now. For the love of grace, please don't ask me again until you're older."

Deeter protested with an uncertain forced laugh, unsure of his father's serious tone and intent. "Dad, we're grown adults in our forties."

The President's face was drawn, "If you aren't one of the few who walk that life with them, if you aren't a man who will willingly send one of them to his death for the good of our country, then you aren't old enough to know yet. Ask me again in eight years."

## FBI Headquarters - Washington DC

The FBI director thumbed through the photographs.

He swallowed back the puke. He sipped some water from a plastic bottle and tried to covertly gargle a little. *Did I hide that well enough? He thought. Do the men think I'm a pussy?*

The field agent ignored his boss's discomfort and continued his briefing, "Sir, these photos depicting a massacre of hundreds, were shared by the New Zealand Intelligence. Their national leadership doesn't know their analysts shared them with us so please consider this classified."

"Their leadership didn't know this was shared?" he asked suspiciously as he fidgeted with his tie, which was his habit when under pressure.

"Sir, their leaders are attempting to cover it up. We suspect they are all compromised by the Chinese. And I think we all know what that means both policy-wise and militarily."

The FBI Director felt more bile rising in his throat. His thoughts were racing... *Shit... do they know I'm compromised too? Are they toying with me?*

He cleared his throat with fake cough sound. "Thank you, please keep me informed of any new developments."

The agent left without a word.

The Director speed dialed Clammer. The CIA Director picked up on the first ring.

"Clammer."

"Did you see?" the Director of the FBI asked.

"What?" Clammer wasn't excited by his half-wit friend's guessing game. He had enough problems of his own with an Inspector General audit of potential security breaches breathing down his neck and a crazy Asian lady threatening him.

The FBI Director lost it and blurted his news like a toddler reporting the need to pee… "New Zealand… they fucking crucified Goldburn… Crucified him... in a tree. They killed everybody… killed the Chinese and left a few hundred dead terrorists on the grounds… I don't know who killed your Burmese terrorists but there must have been at least a thousand Marines to do that."

Clammer scratched his head. How did this dummy become the head of the FBI? "Marines? No way… I'd have heard about it," he lied. "It must be a nation state actor we aren't aware of… How come we aren't aware of it?" He attempted to turn it around on his counterpart.

The FBI Director whined resignedly. "Because we suck… I need to retire and move out of this town immediately."

Clammer held firm. "Not until our, uh… benefactors say it's okay, you aren't… pussy."

The FBI man pushed back, "*You're* a pussy. If we hadn't gone after the President, he might have helped us."

Clammer was obstinate. "He destroyed our little money machine… Fuck him."

"I don't want to get murdered in my sleep by some damned communist. Those tech guys promised we would be part of the survivor class… We were supposed to double-cross and kill the communists with the bug after they made us rich… And now the tech guys are dropping like flies and the commies are all the way up in my ass. Why isn't any of this shit working? Why?" The FBI Director was in a near panic state.

Clammer castigated him. "Shut up, dumbass… keep your mouth shut… we can still pull this off. Just sit tight until you hear from me." Clammer faked his bravado. The FBI Director was the only person he knew that he could occasionally intimidate. But his own fear was taking control of him. He squeaked out an involuntary fart. His stomach hurt. *Why am I always getting screwed?* He contemplated. The CIA Director wasn't done bitching at the FBI man. "We need more men… we have to cover the last of the tech guys. This can still work. My Burmese guys are all dead except for one guy… and he's pissed off. Who do you have?"

The FBI Director thought long and hard before answering. "I got the Iranians."

"Iranians? They hate our guts." Clammer said reproachfully.

The FBI Director expounded, "They might hate your guts, but not mine. Let's just say, we're close. Our old Secretary of State is coordinating with them. I'll have a hundred Revolutionary Guard troops prepared to stage at the perimeter of the next expected target just in case. We need to find out who is hitting these places. They're really pissing off the Chinese."

Clammer sounded pleased. "Good plan." Then he remembered another possible asset. "Hey, I can call our South American desk and see if we can round up a few hundred out of work Venezuelan paratroopers. They are crooked as shit but rather good soldiers otherwise. I mean they aren't at the level of American troops, but they do as they're told most of the time."

"That should be enough to wipe out this '*mystery army*' that is dogging us."

Clammer shifted gears, "I think Berkley Bartson is next."

"The guru of computer-generated graphics?" The FBI Director asked.

"He has Hollywood by the balls and is the top investor in four of the five biggest tech companies. He created a 3D blueprint technology that is being used in building factories that leverages multiple technology disciplines like biology, design, logistics, communication, engineering, kinesics… Complicated as hell but it allows rapid development of massive industrial sites from scratch. He's a big-time democrat donor too."

"No wonder the commies like him. Where is he?"

Clammer explained, "Right now, he's holed up in a massive tea plantation in Chiang Rai, Thailand. He has his own personal Army there… about six hundred security guys. At least he thinks they're his. Most of the security leadership is Chinese."

"Well, with your elite Iranian troops, my cannon fodder commandos from Venezuela, and his guys, that should show a force of about a thousand… Should work. But what if it wasn't him?"

"The three other guys who are still alive aren't as rich, powerful, or smart enough to make a difference. They are just bio-tech lab geeks who struck it moderately rich. They're billionaires, but not major billionaires. They just know stuff, you know, the biological things that they need to pull off the plan… not really influencers. I'm not even sure the enemy even knows who they are. I think the one new geek in the lab in Baja is the only place we might need to cover at some point."

The FBI Director barked, "Don't talk about Baja, dammit. Not on the phone."

"I know. Sorry." Clammer whimpered like a scolded third grader.

The FBI man calmed down. He couldn't risk alienating his counterpart yet. "Well, don't forget. We don't know who the enemy is either. Except for the bastard in the White House."

"Yeah…I know… and therein lies the rub. He's the wild card that could take us all down if we don't get him first."

"I wish the tech guys would release the bio-agent and antidotes and we could get this thing over with. I'm ready for a comfortable island lifestyle."

## THE TOWER RESORT HOTEL — BANGKOK, THAILAND

Mac held a magnifying glass in one hand and a photograph of the massive tea plantation in the other. "There is a shit ton of guys here."

Erika snorted. "I've seen worse."

"So I hear."

"Oh yeah?"

"Yeah, your reputation precedes you."

"Don't believe everything you hear, big guy. The gossips embellish a bit. But so far, we're seeing six hundred guys, and this is just a quick sneak, snoop, whack, and roll operation. We should be gone before these eight balls know we were there."

"Yet somehow it never turns out that way," Mac sighed.

"Third time is the charm."

"Yeah, but this is like the *fourth* time, and the last one wasn't charming... we lost the old man."

Falcone took a more empathetic approach this time. She had already made her point. Now, it was two colleagues talking business, not two strangers establishing the pecking order. She took a sip of beer before responding. "I know you were close... more than just a professional relationship."

"So, you know I have to kill the guy who survived the fight... and the guy who sent him... and the guy he works for, and all of their friends."

"I think that is understood, Mac. I'm in... *if* you want me."

"Copy that."

They clicked beer bottles.

Mac continued. "What happens out there might not be pretty. As a matter of fact, I can guarantee it won't be pretty."

"Oh hell, we'll kill those fuckers... no doubt. We can't let those commie bastards walk. They need to suffer for that shit."

Mac smiled. "Exactly… our partnership has to be based on you understanding that sometimes assholes just die. It's nobody's fault."

"Copy that."

"I just want to honor Pearson… he served his country, his President, and he was my friend."

"I know… and I'm sorry for your loss… but it happens in our line of work. Regrettable, painful, but acceptable. And all we can do is keep moving forward. Let's just gear up and get this job done. After we kill all these knobs, Deeter wants us to deal with a domestic problem stateside next before we do anymore, unless we find the bio-lab… then I bet he'll let us nuke it or something fun."

"Good times." Mac smiled at the thought of nuking something, improving his mood.

"Totally."

They clicked beers again.

He refocused. "Okay fine. Let's run over to the storage locker and pick up our gear."

The pair left the resort, hopped in the Land Rover LR4, and drove through town to the secured warehouse that Mac called the storage locker.

As they arrived at what appeared to be an abandoned factory, Mac touch a button on the dashboard and a large rollup door opened. He drove in, parked, pushed the button again, and closed the door behind them. They exited the SUV and flipped on their flashlights. They walked through the darkness toward the back of the massive building where they encountered a heavy steel door with a biometric reader mounted on the wall beside it. Mac touched it. The door opened. Mac grinned and announced, "Gun City Retail Express is officially opened for business."

There was a large portrait of the President encased in a gold frame centered on the opposite wall, otherwise every square inch of the four-car-garage sized room was lined with weapons. Guns, knives, rifles, flame throwers, machetes, SAWs, shotguns, pistols, rocket launchers, revolvers, and some shit that was so bad ass that it didn't even have a name.

"I think I've found my happy place," Mac whispered as he explored the secret armory.

Erika was impressed. "What is this joint?"

Mac explained as he picked up an M249. "Deeter's personal gun room. He has them all over the world. He likes guns a lot."

"Cool. Me too. I could get used to this," she beamed as she ran her hand over a belt-fed machine gun.

"Let's load up and get to the airport. We're doing an aerial insertion this time, which sucks."

"Especially during monsoon season… in mountains… and a shit ton of hostiles."

Mac noticed that when Falcone discussed overwhelming odds and high-risk situations, she had a weird smile on her face, sort of fiendish… happy, but fiendish… and a look in her eyes that left her appearing a bit deranged. He shrugged in response to her comment about the shit ton of hostiles. "Meh…"

She smiled. "Exactly."

Mac wondered, *is she nuts or just crazy?*

## TEA PLANTATION - CHIANG RAI, THAILAND

Almost immediately the eclectic groups of protective forces arriving around the Plantation caused friction.

"Why must we work with these half-wit Venezuelan banana farmers?" Kabiri ranted as he spoke with the Ayatollah on the satellite phone.

"Watch your tone, Colonel. These filthy infidels are our allies for the moment. Surely you have use for cannon fodder. Just stay hidden on the perimeter and let them absorb the infidels' ammunition, then come in for the kill. Must I explain everything. Do your duty."

"Yes, supreme leader… of course, you are right as always," Kabiri said while thinking *pompous asshole.* Nothing was more frustrating than taking military

186

orders from a fanatical religious lunatic. But inshallah…

"Use them to draw enemy fire… send them on extended patrols… Kill them and booby trap their bodies… there are many ways for these infidels to be useful. Must I make all decisions?"

"Of course not, Supreme Leader. I value your guidance," Kabiri lied. *Swine blood runs through your veins*, he thought.

"Kill whoever threatens our control over America and our intelligence assets there. They must be eliminated. The great Satan does not deserve victory, only humiliation."

"Yes, Supreme leader… it is the will of Allah." *This dirtbag makes me want to puke. What makes him qualified to tell true soldiers what to do?* Kabiri blasphemed freely in his mind with thoughts what would result in instant death if spoken aloud.

"We will kill this tormentor, whoever it is… This is my promise to you." He said solemnly… while thinking, *dickhead. Life in Iran was so much better under the shah.*

\*\*\*

"Why do we have to put up with these goat humping pendejos? We're professional soldiers," Major Franco Moreno complained into his satellite phone.

As long as I'm your handler, you will follow FBI orders. *Your* job is to provide perimeter security for Berkley Bartson and *kill* whoever is murdering these tech guys. You're making plenty of money… do your job."

The FBI SAC disconnected from the call and reported back to the Director. "Sir, the team from Venezuela is in place. They're not happy about their counterparts."

The Director wasn't in the mood for whining communist bullshit. He had enough problems of his own. "Let whoever is coming onto the estate use up their ammo on the Iranians and South Americans. Professional security people will take them down before they breach the inner perimeter.

\*\*\*

"Why are those assholes here?" Bartson's head of security asked again over the satellite phone, dissatisfied with his boss's vague answers.

"They're here to draw enemy fire, Li Wei… That's what Clammer said… he's our man on the inside."

"We can take care of anything they throw at us. I've got enough firepower here to repel the D-Day invasion. So, unless they nuke us from space, we're good… and you control space, right?"

Bartson snickered arrogantly. "Our Space-J project does… and the DoD doesn't even know it."

Li Wie frowned. "Exactly... so once again, why are those assholes here?"

"We have to get along to play along... it's fine. Once our project is launched the FBI, CIA, China, the President... none of them will be a problem again. And with the other group leaders dead, I'll be in charge of the entire planet. Easy street."

Li Wei pretended like he believed Bartson's boasting. He replied with words he thought the technology genius wanted to hear. "Whatever you say, boss." But he thought, *Zhao might think otherwise.*

## THE WHITE HOUSE

The President listened carefully to the woman they called The Fundraiser, although neither she nor her organization never raised funds for him. They were the darkest of the black ops that ever existed. He considered each point she made carefully before speaking, "So, Miss January, let me make sure I have this correct. The Director of the FBI and the Director of the CIA, and probably the Director of National Security are all totally and completely compromised?"

The voice on the secure phone line answered in her usual detailed way. "The three are compromised. Not only compromised, but each of them has sold out as much of their position as possible to as many enemies as possible. In plain terms, they cashed in early and they cashed in often."

The POTUS responded with his perspective, "You know, when they got away with going after that innocent CIA officer, way back in the early nineties, I knew something was wrong. They couldn't find the spy under their nose for twenty years, then they finally arrest a bumbling fool, harassed an innocent man, threatened his family and friends, then gave themselves all promotions. They were probably foreign assets way back then."

The Fundraiser remained objective. "The evidence would indicate that is likely. Shall we handle it?"

The President declined the offer. "No, I'll keep it close to my vest and use my own team. I took the oath of office, it's my job to fix this."

"As you wish, Mr. President. We are available should you request our assistance."

## BANGKOK, THAILAND

Falcone and Mac prepped their gear, loaded it into the helicopter, and said goodbye to the city as they prepared to head for the Northernmost corner of the country.

"McCartney... what the sam hell is that thing?" Falcone asked, pointing at a large canvas bag Mac had stashed over to the side.

"Nothing... Just something I have," he mumbled somewhat elusively.

"Is it that *primary weapon* I've heard so much about?"

"No... absolutely not... But you shouldn't know about that though. It's uh, unpleasant," Mac grumbled a little too defensively.

Falcone shrugged. "Fine. I'm going stock. Four customized Springfield Armory TRP Operator 1911s, my Ka-Bars, an M4, a 590 Shockwave, and an M-60.

"Old school."

"Tried and true."

"The M-60 is a bit dated."

"Some friends of mine swear by them."

"But you can use an M-249, though." he asked, or perhaps stated. It was difficult to tell which by his voice inflection.

Falcone wasn't having it. "You can also stick a corn cob soaked in chili powder up your ass if it makes you happy... I'm sticking with the hog.

"Works for me." Mac capitulated, admiring her brand loyalty.

She turned the tables. "What clubs are in *your* golf bag today, big man?" She asked with a grin.

Mac became serious when talking about his personal firepower. "I'm going with my Wilson Combat AR-10 Ranger, my .500 Smith wheel gun, a couple of desert eagles…"

"44 Mags?"

"Duh."

"Continue," she stated flatly as an accountant reviewing expense reports from the sales force.

Mac resumed outlining his weapons list, "A Barret .50, and uh… one other thing."

"Got it." Falcone didn't press about the one other thing. She had an educated guess as to what it might be from her briefing with Deeter… something awful… and probably banned by most civilized countries in the world. She was one-hundred percent certain it was the primary weapon he just lied about having. *What a sensitive little pussy, won't admit he has a cool toy.*

"Grenades?" Mac asked like a fine diner soliciting menu recommendations from a snooty waiter at a five-star restaurant.

"I recommend five smoke, five flashbangs, one thermite and ten frags… each," Falcone suggested in the uplifting tone of a head waiter fishing for a big tip.

He nodded appreciatively. "Yes, let's go with that… and what if we run into armor?" he inquired further, as if assessing the dessert menu.

Falcone wrinkled up her mouth in deliberation. "Better take a LAWs each. Just to be polite."

"Makes sense. Nothing says *excuse me* like a rocket up the keister."

"Copy that."

The duo fiddled with their gear, cinching down straps, doing a final weapons check, and loading the last of their gear into the spacious bird.

Falcone paused from her work and waited quietly until Mac noticed and gave her his attention. "Mac, I have a question."

"What?"

"Deeter said these missions were supposed to be covert ops with a focus on killing a primary target, making it look like an accident, and then returning to base unnoticed."

"Yeah?"

"Our preparation feels more like a gig where we go in, kill everybody, and burn the place to the ground."

"Yeah?"

"So, is there a part of this that I am missing? I need a job and I don't want to get fired on my first time out for being uh, overenthusiastic."

"Well, I like to look at it like this, Erika," he said, using her given name for the first time. "They take one of ours, we take a thousand of theirs. Besides, the President loves this shit."

"Fair enough."

Their conversation was interrupted by a call on Mac's satellite phone. "It's Deeter."

Mac stepped away to talk the call. The conversation lasted less than thirty seconds. Mac turned his attention back to Erika. "They want us to capture the tech knob alive and find out where the bio-lab is… at all costs."

"Then what?"

"Waste that little bastard and then go the bio-lab and kill everybody."

"Nice."

"Here's his photo. It's the same one from our other packet. Just a refresher in case you spot his ass," Mac said as he handed her the phone.

Falcone studied the face and physical descriptions. *A little bastard, maybe five-five and less than one-hundred-and-thirty pounds. Pasty white…. Stupid expression on his face… Nerd… Not a cool nerd, an annoying nerd.*

Mac looked at his watch. He spoke with fake annoyance. "Hey Falcone, are we going to screw around all day looking at pictures or go to work? It's a quarter till ass-kicking time. Let's roll."

Erika grinned back at him, returned the phone, and climbed into the President's personal Airbus H225 Super Puma and called their pilot, Grayville Lynch IV, on the intercom. "Hit it, Gray."

The helicopter lifted and quickly leveled off, assuming it's cruising speed of about one-hundred-and sixty miles per hour, heading Northbound toward its only fuel stop on the way to the target, Sukhothai Airport.

## ZHAO'S QUARTERS - THE GREAT HALL OF THE PEOPLE - BEIJING

Zhao looked up from his desk as the comrade servant brought him a cell phone on a golden plate.

Zhao picked up the phone. "Hello."

Li Péng, the top operative in the Baja research lab spoke. "Comrade Zhao, in five days the virus will be ready to be disbursed."

"With our modifications?"

"Of course. I saw to it personally. The advanced equipment of the US has given us the weapon we need to assume our rightful place in the world."

"Sole survivors?" Zhao snickered at his joke.

Péng wisely laughed, "Certainly comrade. No more of these filthy Baizuo on the peoples' planet. Complete conquest in six months."

"And they still believe there is an antidote?"

"Yes, comrade. They have no clue that we wrote a new genome code and inserted it into the virus. No non-Chinese will survive. The so-called antidote will just give them a bad case of the flu before they die a horrible death gagging on their own blood."

The thought of dead westerners made Zhao smile. "Carry on, Péng. Let me know when we are ready to launch."

### TEA PLANTATION - CHIANG RAI, THAILAND

Li Wei launched a Skybird Long Range surveillance drone. The device, designed for law enforcement search and rescue, provided a forty-mile range. With five of them he could cover the whole plantation in a matter of hours, making the drone the best method to quickly assess the security status of the sprawling estate.

Today he was focusing on the foreign fighters. His staff didn't trust them. He didn't either. The Iranians were professional soldiers, not great, but good. The South Americans were best at crushing unarmed civilian insurgents and political enemies, not fighting trained US forces. They might slow down the Marines when they come... *but what if it's not Marines who are coming... what if the forces were something else?* He pushed the thought out of his mind. It had to be Marines... *but what other kind of fighting force could do that kind of damage? Seal Team Six? Delta Force? It really wasn't their style. The Marines were the blunt instrument of US military forces.*

After reviewing the pirated US after-action video footage of the carnage from New Zealand and Hawaii, he concluded that there must be at least three hundred Special Forces types involved in these attacks... very ruthless Special Forces types.

There were two long valleys coming down from the hills on the north side of the plantation. He placed the Iranians in one and the Venezuelans in the other... those were the most paths for ingress to the main compound. He had his men formed in an inner and outer perimeter. The outer perimeter was circled by mines. The inner circle had ten pickup trucks with fifty caliber machine guns mounted in the bed. *That should do it. Nobody is taking down this plantation.*

## IN A HELICOPTER OVER NORTHERN THAILAND

"Falcone."

Erika was trying to nap when she heard Mac grunt her name. "What?"

Mac was sprawled on a sofa on the starboard side of the bird looking at a text message on his phone. "When we are done here, I need to go kill a guy. Meet back in Coronado afterwards? I won't be long."

"Sure, Deeter gave me the address and a key. I'll probably stay on my boyfriend's boat in San Diego anyway."

"Sounds good."

Erika suspected what he had in mind and agreed. Certain assholes need to die. She fell back into a deep sleep and forgot about Mac's strange request, notification, rambling, whatever that was.

## White House, Washington DC

The President was not happy. His CIA Director was a spy, the FBI Director was a spy... and how many of their minions were on board with this treason thing? If he had them arrested the country would probably suffer significantly and a jury picked from a Washington DC voter rolls would probably give them a medal instead of jail. The beltway was diseased and crippled. Patriotism and love of country was being replaced with cash payments to government officials at every level.

He hit the intercom button. "Bring my son in, please... and a diet soda... large... and some fries and a burger… make it two burgers. And whatever he wants."

He heard the tinny words through a hidden speaker, "Yes, Mr. President."

The Commander in Chief leaned back in his chair. If one thing business had taught him, particularly the construction business, if things get shitty out there. Don't waste time whining because it can get worse fast.

In a way he felt sorry for these lifetime government employees. They would never get to experience a real success on their own, a private sector success…it's a special feeling when you can look at a building you built, whether you were the CEO or the plumber… it didn't matter. But that thought begs the question, *how did our tech icons get so far off the rails? They're smart guys.*

The only answer he could come up with is that they were just a bunch of total pussies to start with. *There is nothing wrong with that*, he thought. *Until they try to take over the world. They just aren't tough enough for that game. Someone else is involved.*

The door opened and his namesake entered holding a cup of coffee and followed by a steward with a tray bearing his drink and food.

Junior began, "Mr. President. I have some bad news."

"How bad?" the President asked, his full attention on the problem.

Deeter frowned. "Bad for our country, bad for the world. Bad for Mac…. Just bad."

"Where did the intel come from?"

"Mossad. A direct diplomatic dispatch from their Prime Minister."

The President's facial expression went from neutral to grim. "What is it?"

"There's a triple cross in the works and China is behind it. The whole thing is a foreign attack on our way of life."

"Are they certain?"

"Mossad guys are sneaky bastards. I trust them on this."

The President took a long pause before responding. "I do too. Ben knows his business. He was a commando and his brother sacrificed his life fighting these rat bastards. Even people who hate him admit that both men are true heroes in every sense of the word. What do our guys say?"

"It's like we feared. Most of the top-tier guys are in on it at some level or another. We can't find hardly anyone in the beltway upper hierarchy of our CIA, FBI, State Department, or DOJ who aren't corrupted. Another mess to clean up."

"So, all we have is Mossad?"

"I'm afraid so. The State Department has taken point in undermining and selling out our country's interest. Ever since Kennedy let them run rampant over the intelligence community, we have been continuously screwed… so to speak. It's just worse than ever right now."

The President shook his head, revulsed at the level of treason in the swamp. "Let's have it then."

"It looks like this entire world domination plot that the tech gurus hatched, dumb asses that they are, was compromised by the Chinese from the beginning. The People's Republic infiltration into our tech industry is overwhelming. Bottom line, they run our tech companies with the so-called Silicon Valley Giants in place serving as their useful idiots. We were sold out somewhere down the line. Completely and totally sold out."

The President appeared disgusted with the information. "Thanks Bill and Crooked," the President muttered.

"Exactly. So, they have built a biological weapon, using our tech companies, that will cause a mass extinction event for anyone who isn't of Chinese blood. It's extreme gene engineering… weaponized designer biological virus manufacturing that is outlawed by every civilized country in the world."

"How did they develop something like that?"

"They were pretty clever. They set up a bunch of genealogy sites and traced everyone's DNA using the samples that the public voluntarily and enthusiastically submitted. They discovered certain genetic threads that they leveraged to design a specific Chinese genome. After that it was easy to create a delivery system and wipe us all out. I guess you could say we paid them to take our DNA and weaponize it against us. Diabolical."

The President repeated back what he was hearing to confirm his understanding. "So, this bio-weapon will kill everyone on earth but their guys? And all the while, our tech geniuses think they are creating an antidote to a weapon that they can use to kill everyone except their chosen elite?" The President asked, incredulous at the arrogance and stupidity of the Bay Area technology snobs.

His son confirmed. "The Chinese know they can't beat us in a fair fight. So, they use one of our most powerful advantages against us. And most of our incredibly imaginative tech gurus, a bunch of sanctimonious pussies, were so full of themselves that they couldn't imagine someone being smart enough to manipulate them in this way. It all makes sense."

"Assholes!" The President growled. "So foolish and such a waste."

Junior agreed. "Yeah… I'd go ahead and go with *total* assholes. And I don't use that term lightly. I think we all know a total asshole when we see one. They've made moves on our media, science, and engineering space at an incredible rate. It's unacceptable, sir.... In my opinion."

"Can Mac and his new partner fix it?" The First Daughter asked?

Deeter answered. "I think so. They gave us coordinates for the main guy's location... they think the factory is in Mexico someplace... We can end this immediate threat quickly but there is far more work to do beyond just that. There are some more random players to identify, like the people behind Mister Pearson's death, perhaps some Iranian agents out there posing a threat... we don't know all of the players yet but China's rogue leadership must be punished... and we need to deal with our in-house traitors."

"What would old man Pearson do?" the President mused.

His son's gaze turned to steel. "Kill everybody involved and burn all of their shit to the ground... sir. Excuse my language but I believe that's how he would express it."

"I like it. Let's go with that."

# Chapter 11 – Never piss off a lady with a gun

## TEA PLANTATION - CHIANG RAI, THAILAND

The President's helicopter proved to be perfect transportation for Mac and Erika. It dropped quietly from the sky ten miles outside of the outer perimeter of the plantation, allowing its pair of heavily armed passengers to step off into the rolling hills under cover of a starless midnight sky.

Mac McCartney and Erika Falcone moved quickly away from the small clearing into the trees.

Mac watched as the airship left running dark, swiftly ascending into the night and vanishing. He unslung his rifle, lowered his NVGs over his eyes, and gave a quick hand signal to Falcone. The two specialists disappeared, melting into the pitch-black darkness of the rural Thailand landscape.

They moved silently toward the Plantation, closing the gap to the outer perimeter

## WASHINGTON DC

"Clammer. I think they're on to us. What do we do?"

CIA Director Clammer expected that the Director of the FBI would be calling. He wondered what the '*we*' part was all about. Clammer figured he had three potential paths. One, take all the dirty money he'd been paid for thirty plus years and run for a non-extradition country, after faking his death of course. Two, seek asylum in China, where they would probably just torture and execute him after they picked his bones for any useful intelligence that he hadn't already given them. Or three, let this play out and get immunity for testifying against the FBI Director and the rest of their deep state crew.

It occurred to him that there was an opportunity to set the stage for winning back the President's favor. He could let his counter-part draw fire buying him time to formulate either his escape plan or rat plan. He smiled.

"Do you know what I'd do if I were you?" Clammer asked the FBI Director. "I'd get on the TV news and start throwing dirt on the President. Make yourself look like a dedicated public servant. It's not too late to turn this thing around. What's the worst that could happen?" Clammer made this tactical suggestion knowing that the worst that could happen was a military tribunal followed by a lethal injection.

But if he could scam the FBI knob into drawing all the incoming fire, and that egotistical half-witted pious turd would totally do it. Then that might buy the necessary time to get out of this shit. Genius level move.

The FBI Director fell for it. "Smart. I'll get on all the cable talk shows and start pitching my career as a hero and tell everyone how the President is a corrupt nutjob. They'll believe it because they want to believe it."

Clammer smiled as he thought, *draw their fire you big oafish half-wit. I'm out of here at the first possible opportunity!*

## TEA PLANTATION - CHIANG RAI, THAILAND

Mac spotted the first outer-perimeter sniper within two hours of being dropped off by the helicopter. Some a-hole was hiding in a rocky outcropping at the top of a small hill. McCartney held up a fist, stopping their advance, and used hand signals to indicate the sniper position. Then he made a throat slash gesture.

Erika smiled.

Mac got comfortable and drew a bead on the sniper's forehead. He held his fire while Falcone did her thing.

Erika quietly dropped her weapons and ruck before moving with the stealth of a snake to the backside of the hill. Where there was a sniper there was a spotter and maybe even some other jerks. She kept an open mind about what was ahead, avoiding the instinct to speculate and form some preconditioned ideas. This would be an animal style kill, instinctive and brutal.

Within ten minutes she could smell them. Within twelve minutes she could see them. Two teams. One active and one resting. *What a waste of manpower*, she thought... *pussies*.

She withdrew two Ka-Bars and closed. It was time for these assholes to meet the scourge of the desert, the terror of Afghanistan, the knife fighter... Erika Falcone, USMC retired.

She was positioned between the on-duty sniper and his spotter before they even realized she was there. They were both dead before they could react... one speared through the temple and the other in the back of the neck in a simultaneous attack. She posed in a deep martial arts style stance as the thick red blood dripped slowly off the blades of the massive knives as she waited to see if there was any response from the last two men.

She mouthed the word, 'Murica!' then moved to the two sleeping assholes. They were both laying on their backs, unaware of the imminent threat. Falcone shifted her stance, turning at the hips one-hundred and eighty degrees and raising her hands high before jamming a Ka-Bar into an eye of each of her targets, burying the knives to the hilt through their heads. She stood on their chests and yanked the blades out of the dead men's melons. She wiped down the blades on their shirts and returned to Mac's position, smiling and incredibly grateful that this awesome job had been offered to her and that she had accepted. Good times ahead.

Mac saw her appear again through the rocks. She gave him a quick *let's advance* hand signal. They moved on to the next targets. He didn't like it. Time wasn't on their side or they could wander around aimlessly and killing people all night… there were just too many of them to be able to finish the gig by dawn using this method. *Fun? Yes… Efficient? No. What would Pearson do?*

Mac took point, leading the way up through the hills until they came to the peak that divided into to two winding valleys. They stopped to observe and take a short break and to do a visual recon of the plantation from the vantage point. The maps were correct, the only two paths of ingress were the pair of narrow valleys leading down to the somewhat level bottom land of the plantation.

Falcone popped one of the hydrators into her mouth as she waited for Mac's assessment. The hydrator units were something new that was added to their kits. Each hydrator unit looked sort of like a blue laundry detergent pod, but they were filled with alkaline water infused with electrolytes. It was the equivalent of consuming eight ounces of water. The benefit was it was lighter than carrying water, more silent than carrying water, and more efficient than water. Plus, it tasted good. Still, Erica carried a couple of small water bottles in her pocket in the event of a situation. *Tech is fine but water is for more than just drinking.*

Mac continued scanning the area with the high tech monocular Deeter had provided to them which made their old pirated DARPA optics seem like kids' toys. Mac whispered into his comm unit, "Look up there."

Falcone used her monocular to see what he spotted. She whispered, "Drones."

"Drones suck." Mac grumbled.

"Yeah. They'll see us coming."

Mac switched his monocular to thermal. "Shit."

"What?" Falcone asked, using the word most often used after hearing someone say *shit*.

"About a trillion assholes are staged in these two valleys."

"A trillion?" She said skeptically. A trillion seemed like a lot of assholes.

"More than one, less than a trillion… somewhere in that range... Maybe a few hundred guys." Mac suspected that Falcone now knew that math wasn't his best thing.

She dismissed the concern. "No biggie."

"But how do you explain the wide gap of no man's land between the guys in the valley and the perimeter at the plantation house?"

"Mine field?" she suggested.

"That would make the most sense."

"Land mines suck too."

Mac felt like Falcone was on the same page with him now on this whole recon business. "I know, right?" Vague is always good enough when you know that any refined plans will turn to shit as soon as the operation is launched.

Falcone presented an idea. "So… let's try this. I'll take one valley. You take the other valley. We kill everybody and see if they have something we can use to blast a path through the mine field. We meet at the convergence and then we breach their perimeters and kill everybody inside."

Mac smiled. Finally, a plan that was easy to follow, wasn't restrictive, and was based mainly on luck and guts. "I like the creative elements of this plan. Let's give it a shot. It might be fun."

"What about the drone?"

"Well, when we take down the main house, we'll grab the video and add it to our greatest hits collection. If we do our job, it won't matter what they see. But if you get a chance, take 'em out."

Falcone gave a thumbs up. It sounded good to her. This pre-raid recon was a cakewalk.

Mac popped a hydration pod in his mouth. He held up his hand with fingers extended giving a visual countdown. *Five, four, three, two, one. Kill time.*

## ZHAO'S QUARTERS - THE GREAT HALL OF THE PEOPLE - BEIJING

Zhao smiled. Now only three days left until the virus was released. Within six months, everyone on the planet who was not Chinese would be dead. The secret facility set up by the useful idiot tech gurus was wrapping up the production of the bioweapon. If no one discovered the location of the bio-weapon lab and intervened, he would soon overthrow the Party Chairman President Lu and then install himself as Emperor of the world. But what kind of maniacs would be able to find this location and destroy it? Only the Directors of the CIA and FBI could fill in those blanks for the Americans. He'd need to eliminate them... he'd send Kang... Kang could suicide them, as he did so many times previously for Zhao by neutralizing the renegade American assets. It was much easier back in the days when he owned the American Presidents… The new guy though was a wild card. His unbridled support for his own country's interests was infuriating. Still… the mission at hand was to protect the lab, not exploiting further corruption in the Washington bureaucracy.

Without the United States knowing Berkley Bartson was the front man for the biological warfare lab, they would need to capture him and make him give up the facility's secret location in Baja, Mexico. But he was too well protected in his remote South East Asia location. Still, perhaps it would be a responsible move to send paratroopers to reinforce his position.

Zhao made a call to The Chinese People's Liberation Army headquarters and gave the order. "Prepare a thousand elite paratroopers for deployment to Northern Thailand."

General Li squirmed in his chair. He had ten thousand men at his disposal, but none of them were elite. And none of them were paratroopers. And his planes were broken down old junk.

"Elite paratroopers, sir?" he asked, hoping he misunderstood the order.

"Yes, send our top commandos. Only the best of the best."

"Yes, sir." Li didn't want to become one of the infamous conference table target practice victims that

Lao was known for executing. He disconnected the call and stared blankly out the window. *We have some fifty-year-old parachutes, some dumbasses… some planes…. I can make it work.*

Forty miles away in his office, Zhao smiled. The threat would be handled with brute force by elite troops. *More than sufficient manpower is assigned,* he thought. *What could possibly go wrong now?*

He dialed his personal number for Kang the Assassin… the most dangerous man he had ever met and the most useful tool in his arsenal against the western corruption investigations that chronically plagued the Chinese hundred-year plan. It was time to clean up the trail of American traitors.

## TEA PLANTATION – CHIANG RAI, THAILAND

Erika bypassed the Venezuelans on the outer perimeter. They were obviously not good enough to bother with killing right off the bat. She crept further down the sloping valley to the core of the Iranian inner perimeter, only pausing to plant claymores along the trail behind her for those South American commie bastards when they come… and commie bastards always come. That was one trait for sure about them, they never quit coming at you. Erika also left a fifty-pound satchel charge stuffed with twenty pounds of 16D common framing nails behind her, a little package Mac taught her how to prepare. *I love remote detonators*, she thought as she set the deadly charges. She was also glad to lighten her load significantly by dispersing the booby traps to cover her ingress into the Iranian compound.

The Iranians were more disciplined than their Venezuelan buddies, which wasn't saying much. She knew their style. Whenever she worked in Iraq, she found the Ayatollah's rat bastard pets from hell to be a chronic pain in the neck. Mediocre soldiers, annoying as hell. Not to mention that they needed killing for being total assholes… and they would be predictably reckless once the shit hit the fan. *Nice*.

She checked her equipment before she engaged. Her M4 had the PMAG D60 drum magazine and she had two more drums ready to rock in ammo pouches. The pair of heavy Colt Special Combat Government Model 45s in her favorite belt configuration, one in right hand draw, one in left hand cross draw, felt familiar and comforting. The 590 Shockwave was slung on her back and the hog, an old M60 belt fed machine gun, just like the one her boyfriend gave her for an engagement present, was held lovingly in her hands. The M60 was a weapon she came to admire from her association with the legendary Guts Gutterman, the best Marine she ever worked with. Last, but not least, was her beloved Ka Bars, held against her body in a shoulder holster rig, ready to go full balls out Sushi Chef mode on the commies as needed.

The load out was heavy as hell but Erika had a theory about that. If your load is too heavy, then get in better shape or get right into the shit and start killing people. Burning through the ammo always lightens the load… or do both… that's called multi-tasking.

She took a slug of water before walking down the hill to kill everyone in her path. It's always best to stay hydrated.

Time to play… she smiled as she hoisted the M60 and began her trek down the slope into what was soon to become a walk through the valley of the shadow of death for a shit ton of America-hating bastards.

## East Valley – Outer perimeter of the Tea plantation - Chiang Rai, Thailand

Mac moved to the top peak above the small valley he intended to take down. He was far enough back to be out of the flight path of the drones and there were no more sentries or snipers about. *All good.*

He initiated his descent.

He thought he heard the faint echoes of a belt-fed machine gun and death screams from the adjoining valley.

"Don't get greedy, Falcone. Save some for me," he grumbled.

Suddenly, a random patrol of five dirtbags crashed through the tall brush on the right, sprinting across open ground just ten yards from Mac, but not noticing him. Apparently, they were scrambling towards the sound of gunfire... *or maybe these shitheads are just scrambling because they are shitheads and that's what shitheads do. It doesn't matter. Shitty unit discipline you got there, assholes*, he thought before he yelled at them, "Hey!"

The five stopped and turned to see who shouted just in time for each of them to catch a three-round burst of fire in the kissers. The can on Mac's rifle minimized the sound of the report to the immediate area.

*Five up and five down.*

Mac continued down the trail towards the mine field, moving carefully through the rocky terrain. At this distance he could no longer hear his partner firing. He did a quick comm check in with Falcone... she was fine. He continued.

"Oh shit!"

In a narrow side canyon, apparently out of earshot of Falcone's carnage, a small encampment of about two hundred men were noisily gathered around a food delivery truck. The truck was a battered four wheel-drive Japanese import with an improvised cargo rail around the bed made from old wooden shipping pallets. A burly Asian man stood in the bed and was tossing out brown bagged lunches and bottled waters to the bored and inattentive security team who played grab ass and chattered away while they waited their turn for chow.

Mac heard them speaking Spanish… He frowned… Venezuelan commandos? Pussies. He saw them eating sandwiches and potato chips. *They have American food…. Assholes… but you know… I could eat*, he thought. He loaded one of his custom-built double-drum one-hundred round magazine into the Wilson Combat AR-10 Ranger and charged his weapon.

He stood up. It was time to start this show. "Guess who's coming to dinner, assholes!" he shouted.

The unruly men surrounding the truck ignored him, assuming one of their colleagues was acting out… military decorum was out the window with the poorly disciplined Venezuelans. They appeared to be in vacation mode rather than on high alert. No one even noticed his presence.

Mac sat back down… *Well shit… that was rude.* He fished a fragmentation grenade out of a cargo pants pocket. He pulled the pin and let the spoon spring away. He threw it as high and hard as he could toward the gathering. It detonated above their heads raining shrapnel into the crowd.

Mac shouldered the AR-10 and fired into the chaos like he was intending to melt down the barrel.

Instead of dispersing out into the jungle, the Venezuelans inexplicably began crowding around the truck. They returned fire randomly into the surrounding bushes and trees as Mac sustained fire into the densest mass of them that he could see.

Mac burned down the enemy by the dozens as he emptied the first hundred rounds into the commie assholes. He smoothly dropped the empty magazine and reloaded his rifle with a smaller Magpul fifty round drum, saving the three remaining big drums in his ruck for later, just in case things got serious. He estimated half of the group was down and all the survivors seemed disoriented and confused. *They must have pussies for NCOs*, Mac thought. With the initial onslaught complete, he could now start moving and selecting targets more discreetly.

He cut to the left towards some trees. Mac effectively leveraged cover as he fired, occasionally pausing and going for head shots when there was an opportunity.

The disorganized mob of mercenaries he was murdering was unable to form up an organized resistance. Mac frowned as he assessed his immediate enemy. They were just over-rated socialist scum; all talk and no unit discipline. *It's a pleasure to kill them.*

Mac paused when he heard an earth-shaking explosion in the other valley. "what the hell kind of racket it that?" he muttered. *Probably Falcone is exploding shit...* He grinned as he considered the sound further. *No... definitely, Falcone exploding some shit.*

---

## WEST VALLEY — OUTER PERIMETER OF THE TEA PLANTATION - CHIANG RAI, THAILAND

Falcone moved in on a group of about forty Republican Guard radical Islamic assholes gathered in a clearing. It looked like shift change at a fast food joint. *These guys are pathetic*, she observed as she let the M60 do its thing. The distinctive sound was beautiful music to her ears, but the Iranians were not enjoying it. They folded like unstarched laundry. Bloody, chopped to pieces laundry, but definitely folded laundry.

She continued the barrage as more soldiers rushed from the bush and into the fray of the little clearing.

The word slaughter came to mind as Erika moved and fired. Then she heard the explosions behind her. The dipshit Venezuelans must be coming to the rescue and stumbling into all her trip wires.... *hahahaha... so funny.* But Erika hadn't even hit the good stuff yet. That shit was all connected to remotes. This was fun.

Falcone was a fearsome beast hidden in the body of a beautiful super model who was dressed to kill… The 5.11 military style pants in black but cut off below the knee like capri pants, Saloman Quest tactical boots, a dark green cotton tank top and her favorite black boony hat, did little to conceal the sexual steaminess of her muscular build, long brown hair, and more than ample cleavage. Her muscles glistened in sweat as she hefted a fifty-pound ruck and the heavy load bearing vest. She had near perfect facial features other than a slight vertical scar between her right eye and ear that she picked up in a Panama knife fight. Of course, her opponent from that fight had a slight scar that ran from his nuts to his throat that left his bleeding remains twitching in the dirt. So… that was nice. She felt like the scar gave her character. Some women have a mole or a dimple… Erika sported battle scars.

She took a position of cover behind a rock outcropping to feed another belt into the hog. She heard more troops crashing through the brush perhaps a quarter mile up the slope. It must be the rest of the Iranian and Venezuelan mercs for this valley.

She heard a quick squelch and then Mac's voice in her ear comm… "what do you have?"

She responded, "It looks like a shit ton of dirtbags are heading up my side, but they seem to be running on herd instinct and are forming into a large mob of enemy maggots. I got some of them coming up the hill and the ones I passed are behind me coming down the hill."

"Copy enemy maggots from multiple directions. I'm running out of assholes to kill over here. I'll move back up to the ridge so I can help if you need it."

"I'm good."

"Are you sure?"

"Take cover, Mac… it's about to get real western out here."

Erika removed her ear comm and retrieved her ear plugs from a pocket in her load bearing vest, stuffing one in each ear. She dug the remote detonator for the satchel charge out of another pocket and waited. Below her the surviving Iranian troops from the first bunch dug in… maybe twelve of them alive and functioning. But above her she sensed about seventy assholes rushing down the trail. She concentrated, attempting to determine exactly where they would intersect with her satchel charge…. Close… Close… there.

She punched the button and the explosion rocked the hillside. *Shit!* For a moment she thought she set off an atomic bomb by accident. Shit flew everywhere and she tumbled down the hill into the midst of the dozen Iranians she hadn't killed yet. Luckily, they were busy shitting their pants as debris and body parts rained down on them from above. Mud, blood, brush, jungle, rocks, and 16D framing nails shot through the air as shrapnel, ripping apart anything and everything unfortunate enough not to be behind some kind of protective cover.

Erika tumbled into a ditch and avoided the blast.

She started laughing as she scanned the results her unanticipated extended blast radius. *Whoops!*

Dead guys were strewn across the hillsides. *Maybe I used too much C4*, she pondered… then she remembered something Gutterman once told her. *Nah, there's no such thing as too much explosive material.*

Falcone realized that in the chaos there were some Iranians nearby who weren't very dead. In fact, they looked pretty healthy. Six of them had taken cover in the same ditch she was in and they were not only healthy but pissed off. Luckily, they had dropped their guns while escaping  the blast. Unfortunately, they had knives. Unfortunate for them.

Erika smiled. She was in her happy place. Being surrounded by assholes in a knife fight was so charming. She pulled her Ka Bars and grinned at the prospects of gutting these radical-assed fuckers.

Iranians love martial arts… all the young males seem to be into some form of hand to hand combat training. Many of them are into the most flamboyant or flashy styles, and often the trendiest new styles. Erika knew this. But she also knew that this was an advantage for her. They wouldn't rush her for a quick takedown. They would each underestimate her and try to use their most glitzy move. She could easily kill each of these guys with minimal effort.

She stood in a low balanced stance, watching as guy number one tried some stupid high strike with his right hand then spin into a low reverse sweep with his right leg. Basic stuff. Erika slipped the strike, stepped over the sweep, and stabbed him in the throat with a quick jab. He looked surprised as he clutched his throat and fell backwards twitching on the ground.

Guy number two did the standard flying side kick he had probably admired in so many martial arts movies and had mastered through hundreds of repetitions in front of his fawning peers at the karate studio over the years. He went high. Erika went into a deep low stance and stabbed him in the nuts with the left-hand knife as he flew over her in his perfect form. He went straight down like a shit bucket tossed out of a Bombay tenement house window. She shifted to the left and opened his throat with the right-hand knife. He quit fighting.

The other four survivors realized at this point that they were in a knife fight with somebody who was serious about the killing business. They led with their blades.

Erika deflected jabs, parrying them away with ease as she enjoyed the sizzling sound of steel on steel. She found it relaxing.

The tallest of the four original attackers lunged in for the kill from directly behind Falcone.

Erika sensed the attack, heard the shuffling of feet behind here, and adjusted her stance almost imperceptibly to her right. The man's knife blade ripped the fabric of her tank top but didn't find skin. His hand extended past her body as he had put all his weight behind the thrust of the blade.

*A miss is as good as a mile.* She slashed down with a brutal swipe and almost cut the attacker's hand off with her scalpel sharp battle knife. He shrieked in pain and fell to his knees clutching his ruined appendage. Erika ignored him for the moment while she deflected slashing blades from the two in front of her. She parried the blades to the outside of her body line, stepped in between them and with a crossing move, buried a knife in each of their ears.

A scream from the right came from the fourth guy. He charged in wide-eyed and crazy with his knife held in both hands high above his head.

Erika smiled. *Ain't that special.* Falcone gracefully executed a front shoulder roll at a forty-five-degree angle from the attack as she simultaneously slid her shotgun out of the leather pouch across her back, deftly racked a shell into the chamber, and pumped a twelve-gauge rifled slug into the side of his head. The forward momentum of the attack carried the now headless knife wielder forward where he tumbled in a heap on top of his dead friends.

Then the real shit went down.

## East Valley — Perimeter of the Tea plantation - Chiang Rai, Thailand

Mac was having a ball. He was kicking ass and stacking bodies of dirtbags who hated America… his happy place. But he was running low on dirtbags. The only thing that could make this day better was if he could have a pint of cold beer and a cigar… *Wait… I got a cigar.* He retrieved the Arturo Fuente Hemingway Signature in Maduro and carefully removed it from his custom ballistic DeBlasio tactical cigar holder. He cut it with his Xikar XO gun metal gray cigar cutter and lit it with his Vertigo torch. Mac took a long drag before advancing again down the sloping valley.

He found another clearing and took a moment to glass the area. About a thousand yards away on the ridgeline connecting the two valleys, a few straggler Republican Guard troops were scrambling down the slope, probably escaping the claymores and satchel charge drama. *Falcone must have spanked these clowns good,* he thought. Mac unslung his Barrett and lined up the first shot. *Might as well relax for a moment.* The big rifle roared and bucked into his beefy shoulder. In the scope he could see a bad guy blown to pieces by the six-hundred plus grain fifty caliber round that ripped into him at about twenty-seven-hundred feet-per second… The rest of the stragglers turned and started running back over the ridge… they'd had enough of Mister Barrett's neighborhood. Mac scanned for threats and advanced again… when suddenly, things got ugly.

## WEST VALLEY - – PERIMETER OF TEA PLANTATION - CHIANG RAI, THAILAND

Falcone stared wide eyed at the sky full of parachutes. *Paratroops? A shit ton of paratroops? Who in the hell are these assholes? There must be a thousand of them.*

She touched her ear comm unit and spoke, "Mac… are you seeing this shit?"

Mac responded, "You mean flying assholes in the sky?"

"Yeah… A lot of them and they're still coming… Must be twenty planes coming in dropping sticks. Who are they?"

"Stand by…"

She waited for a full minute before Mac came back on the air. "Deeter confirms they aren't ours and they don't belong to the Thai military… consider them hostiles. But there does seem to be a lot of them."

"The more the merrier."

"Copy that… meet me at the top of the ridge… and bring the hog. Chop Chop."

"On my way."

She noted that these guys opened their chutes from a high altitude. They might have been deployed from some transports doing a static line jump. It seemed fishy… maybe these weren't elite paratroops. Perhaps they were just cannon fodder attached to parachutes. Erika decided she it didn't matter… she'd just kill them all.

She powered her way up the sloping valley to the steep ridgeline that separated her and Mac, quickly meeting him at the rendezvous as the slowly drifting parachutes rained down from the clouds.

Mac was grinning wide and toothy… "Hold my beer."

"You don't have any beer."

"Figure of speech."

Mac lined up the Barrett 50 and targeted aircraft. "This isn't really as easy as I'm going to make it look so save your applause for the end."

"Copy that."

"And when these incoming assholes are in range, light 'em all up with the 60."

"You have no idea how long I've waited to hear those words."

"Let's rock."

Mac sighted in a slow flying and low altitude aircraft.

Falcone spoke up, "I have the couple hundred or so almost on the deck about three hundred yards down the ridge."

Mac ripped a three-round burst of fifty BMG before answering. "Hit it."

Falcone ran a belt through the M60 into the dense field of floating parachutes drifting in at less than two hundred feet above the ground. The rounds ripped the vulnerable troops to pieces. But more were coming behind them. She carefully but quickly loaded another belt. "Moving in twenty yards closer."

"Move."

Falcone heard sputtering as a damaged aircraft lost power and then burst into flames. She heard another short burst of fifty BMG. Another aircraft swerved in the sky into a larger plane that had not yet dropped the paratroops.

"How in the hell is he doing that? That's impossible." Falcone muttered before she lit up the next batch of parachutes approaching the ridge. They killed about one hundred and fifty guys so far in her estimate. She counted about four hundred effective enemy on the ground forming up to counterattack. *That's bad news*, she thought as she continued firing… *Worse news… They are still coming. Hey! Good news…* She noticed the fiery hulk of the second plane Mac shot heading towards the enemy troops, burning brightly like a meteor hitting the atmosphere, and there was now another one coming down right behind it. *Damn!*

Mac continued targeting the aircraft. He got one more. He touched his ear comm and announced, "They're turning back to asshole town… or wherever assholes come from." He gave a running commentary as he began targeting clusters of chutes. "Our guys would have probably used helicopters and hot roped in or done a HALO drop…. They definitely wouldn't be using a bunch of old World War Two training chutes. Whoever oversaw equipping and training these guys was a dick."

"Copy that. I'm moving down to take out stragglers. There could still be a hundred of them wandering around on the ridge in the brush."

229

"I'll join you. Whoever is coming is on the ground now… and I bet they aren't real happy."

Mac slung the heavy rifle and switched to his carbine. He smiled as he watched Falcone use the custom sling to carry the heavy M60. *She is strong as fuck*, he thought as they advanced toward the enemy. He noticed she switched to a shotgun instead of her M4. *Nice… in this brush that will work out fine.* He heard her whisper in the comm unit.

"I'll take point. Cover me… We'll flush these spank wieners out."

"Copy that," Mac answered, still grinning. *This is fun.* "What is that little jewel you're carrying, Falcone?"

"My shotgun? I call it OSKAR. One-Shot-Kill-And-Repeat. I load it with slugs, so I don't have to shoot somebody twice." She grinned an evil smile, "Never make me repeat myself, Mac. It pisses me off." She gave him a knowing wink.

Mac shook his head. "I'm sorry could you say that again? I wasn't listening."

"Asshole." Falcone snorted a laugh. "If I wasn't carrying a heavy-assed armory, I'd flip you off."

The pair threaded their way along the ridge towards the main plantation compound, swerving wide of the fires spreading from the downed planes and avoiding stepping on the crispy critters littering the ground.

## OFFICE OF THE DIRECTOR OF CENTRAL INTELLIGENCE

The Director of the CIA Clammer was not really a spy and not really a cop and not even much of a bureaucrat. He liked to think of himself as an entrepreneur. Reclining back in his ten-thousand-dollar office chair with his feet propped on the desk he reflected on his years of service. His career was at least interesting if not exciting. Originally hired by the agency as an FOIA attorney he worked his way up the food chain, eventually spending most of twenty-five years at CIA dealing with awkward litigation and difficult litigants in HR. Over the years he cleaned up enough messes that he enjoyed a significant level of influence, which he used to his advantage. Knowing where the embarrassing bodies were buried was an effective tool for climbing the ranks in a government job. His one dream was to get out of the USA and find a chateau in France for retirement. He would hire someone to write his memoirs and burn every jerk who ever disagreed with him during those seemingly endless Washington years. The Chinese promised a fat paycheck when he retired... and now... it was all turning to crap... all because the President wouldn't play the games that everyone else did.

His reverie was broken by an alert on his cell phone. He read the screen. It was the Director of the FBI. He took the call with an abrupt, "What?"

The head of the FBI bleated out, "Clam Man… Everything is turning to total shit."

Clammer thought the FBI man might be crying… or at least sniveling. *Oh yeah. He's totally sniveling.* He answered vaguely, not ready to share information with Clammer. "I heard. How bad?" Clammer was lying. He hadn't heard anything.

"I don't know… they killed about a million guys… there must be a full division with armor and air support taking down the Tea Plantation. It's a massacre. We got to get everyone out of Baja while there is still time… before they find that shithole and have us all executed for crimes against humanity."

"We don't talk about Baja! Not on the phone." The CIA Director scolded his whiny counterpart. Clammer attempted to sound authoritative but he felt himself starting to snivel. He was losing it. *Those Chinese bastards! That Orange bastard… Why can't everyone just take the money and play the game?* A slightly damp fart escaped his bowels with a squeaky toot. He squirmed a little in his seat to adjust his shorts.

The Director of the FBI pressed. "We need to leave town."

Clammer dismissed the idea. "Waste of time. They've already been here and told me we need to hold fast."

"They came to see you too? Who was it?"

"Some random Asian lady... she scared the shit out of me. How did she even get in my office past security? Why does she talk like she's from Alabama? That's not how communists sound." Clammer commiserated.

"She was in your office? Oh nooooo!!!! The FBI Director bayed woefully as a hound that just attempted to boink a porcupine. The Director's mind raced. *Clammer probably spilled his guts to save his own ass. Jerk!*

Through the phone, Clammer overheard a tinny voice speaking over an intercom in the FBI Director's office.

"Your appointment is here, sir," the voice announced pleasantly.

He heard the Director answer, "I don't have an appointment."

Clammer shouted into the phone, "That's her... that's how she got me."

He heard the Director of the Bureau squeal like he was goosed with a foot-long frozen kielbasa.

"Shiiiiit!"

The line went dead. The call disconnected.

Clammer sat motionless with the vacant eyes of a death row inmate on judgement day, his thoughts drifting to imminent doom. *Shit. That worm will spill his guts and get us all killed.*

## North side - Inner-Perimeter of the tea plantation mansion - Chiang Rai, Thailand

Falcone picked up a dead guys arm that still had a sleeve on it to wipe the blood off her Ka Bar. She tossed the arm away when she finished and sheathed the blade in her custom leather rig. She yelled across the field. "Mac… I killed all of mine… try to keep up." She could only see his head above the mound of dead bodies surrounding him.

McCartney kicked over the stack of dead maggots between them so he could walk to her position and wouldn't have to shout.

"Ammo?" he asked as they met in the middle of their killing fields

Erika shrugged. "It's time to pick up what we can off these assholes. I've used almost everything I brought."

"I still got some rounds for the fifty, but otherwise I'm a little low myself."

"We might need that again before we're through with this shit," She agreed.

"Then let's get to it. It's time to breach the inner perimeter and kill that little prick."

"Copy that. I'm switching to one of their AKs and filling my ruck with mags."

Mac started searching bodies for ammo. "Me too… they didn't come well prepared. I found a few grenades. But nothing cool."

"Did you use your primary weapon?" She asked. "I didn't hear it."

"No. I didn't bring that one. Things aren't that ugly yet."

"True. But the day isn't over yet either."

## THE WHITE HOUSE – WASHINGTON DC

Deeter picked up the porcelain coffee pot and topped off his sister's cups as he explained the news. "Our field team is about to clear the Tea Plantation Headquarters. That will end that immediate threat. I am hopeful someone will be left alive to tell us where the bioweapon lab is located though.

"Well, without the old man to keep them in check, I wouldn't be surprised if they just shoot first and forget about asking questions," the President remarked as he sipped his diet soda.

The First Daughter replied, "These… people of violence… Mac and Falcone. They seem to step up as the risk escalates. I'm not concerned about them. They'll get the information we need."

"What about the Myanmar wild card we got the tip on?" The President asked.

"I asked Mac to kill them last. He wasn't happy but he agreed."

"Good…. But make sure he kills them all. We can't have random warlords killing Americans and believing they will live to gloat about it. I can call in a missile strike."

"I think Mac will do more damage than a missile strike. Let's let that one play out and finish this lab thing. Clearly the Chinese think we won't find it in time and destroy it."

The President nodded in agreement. "I'll take care of the Chinese issue after the lab is gone. It's time they got with the program."

"Nuke them?" The First Daughter asked.

"I'm not taking that off the table," the President said grimly. "But I have a swamp to clean up first. There are some traitors here at home who need crushed, big league… crushed like the corrupt bugs that they are. *That*, I can tell you. They're a disgrace, horrible people."

## THE GREAT HALL OF THE PEOPLE - BEIJING

Zhao screamed at them sitting around the conference table, "What happened? Why are these elite troops dead? Why are the American Forces still advancing?"

"Director Zhao," the head of the assassin program whispered nervously. "Those troops we sent weren't that elite… they were what we had available. The planes we used were old and slow. I tried to tell you."

Zhao jerked the pistol from out of his jacket and shot the man in the guts… "Die slowly, coward!"

The man jerked twice in his chair before slumping to the floor where he lay twitching for almost five minutes. No one spoke.

Zhao screamed in rage, "Get Li Wei on the phone!"

Aids scrambled to fulfil the volatile leader's wishes.

Moments later Zhao held a phone to his ear, speaking with Bartson's head of security. "Wei, what is your situation."

The normally calm Li Wei sounded frightened. "There have been terrible explosions and loss of life. It's a massacre. We estimate that at least five thousand American troops are coming down out of the highlands. We only have about six hundred men left. We need to evacuate."

Zhao was infuriated. "No… stay and fight."

"But, sir… "

Zhao cut him off. "Fight, you coward. The American's can't take Bartson into custody. He can reveal the locations of national security facilities we can't allow them to find. We're close enough that we can complete the project without him now if we have to."

"Sir, we can't hold out long."

"Stand fast. We are sending additional support. You shouldn't have to wait long."

"Yes, sir." Li Wei said… "How long?" His low confidence in timely support arriving given away by his tone.

"Soon… Real soon."

Zhao disconnected the call and addressed his attention to the senior general of the military. "I need a guided missile directed into the Tea Plantation Mansion within the next fifteen minutes."

"We have a submarine in the area that can handle that immediately, sir." The General answered warily.

"Good… make it happen."

## TEA PLANTATION MANSION - CHIANG RAI, THAILAND

*We're dead men*, Lie Wei thought as he put the phone back in his pocket.

Li Wei grabbed Bartson by the collar and pointed to his five best shooters, "You... You... You... You two... On me."

The highly trained security operatives formed a stack and followed Li Wei and their client to the escape tunnel .

Li Wei led the way using a flashlight to navigate the crude tunnel system under the main house. He wasn't happy as his thoughts wandered to his real boss back in China. *Zhao is a dick.*

## TEA PLANTATION - CHIANG RAI, THAILAND – BEYOND THE INNER PERIMETER

Mac and Falcone proceeded to the inner perimeter of the compound. From behind a large rock formation he scanned the base with his field glasses. He noted five-foot-tall block walls surrounded the complex and defense forces lined the fortification spaced about 10 feet apart. There was a clear kill zone outside the wall of about 200 yards.

"I'm not liking this very much. We're gonna have a hell of a time getting across that open area without getting killed in the process. It's probably mined and they're ready for us."

"I wish we could call in an airstrike," Falcone muttered in response, when suddenly an ear-piercing scream of what sounded like a jet engine flew over their head.

Then the earth shook. A concussive thud preceded an intense bright light then immediate darkness as wind equivalent to a force five tornado swept the land.

Despite the rocky cover between them and the blast scene, Mac and Falcone flew backwards over 20 yards, bouncing off the landscape like plastic toys before being enshrouded in a massive dust cloud. Mack was completely disoriented. Between the force of the blast and the dense dust cloud enveloping him, he could not determine what direction he was facing. His ears were ringing from the explosion and his eyes were encrusted with dirt and debris… *Where was Falcone?* He collapsed into unconsciousness.

Erika Falcone picked herself up from the deck. She couldn't hear. She touched her right ear with her index finger. It came back bloody. "Mac, what the fuck was that?" She said but she couldn't hear her own words, just a piercing high-pitched ringing.

Erika remembered her training. When in doubt, get to cover and assess your surroundings… prepare for the worst. Keep your guard up. She low crawled into a slight dip in the terrain that might have been a trench or a creek bed before the blast and waited for the sky to clear. *If Mac is dead, he'll have to deal with that shit himself*, she thought. Reaching into a cargo pants pocket she fished out a small bottled water and used it to rinse her eyes clear before washing out her mouth. She sat upright with her rifle at the high ready, prepared to engage enemy combatants should any of those rat bastards still be alive. *Bring it, assholes!*

As the dust cleared, Erica initiated a grid search for Mac. She found him slammed against a tree stump with a bloody nose and blood coming from his ears. She used the remainder of her bottled water to rinse his eyes. Slowly he began to come around.


"Mac, what the sam hell was *that* shit? Did we just get nuked?"

Mac's brain and mouth kicked into gear before his body did. Between coughs he answered as best he could. "I have *no* idea what the hell that was about. As close as I can tell we were just blown the fuck up... But we need to go find our guy, or at least find his body. Mission comes first. We still don't know where the lab is. Can you walk?" He began his first attempt at getting to his feet. Fail. He sat for a moment.

Falcone rolled her neck and stretched her shoulders. "I think I'm good to go."

"Then let's get out of here and find that guy." Mac stood this time and headed into the compound grounds, or what was left of it. The dirt in the air gave him a coughing fit. He popped a hydrator unit in his mouth. He hacked out some dirt spit on the ground seconds later.

Erika Falcone had seen her fair share of destruction during her time in the Marine Corps and even during a couple of side gigs in Arizona and

Mexico… But she was stunned at the level of destruction here. "Man… this is bad." The entire site was reduced to smoking rubble. There were unidentifiable lumps that might have been bodies at the outer edges of the blast zone. "This looks like a MOAB strike, but it was a missile-based delivery… who in the hell has that kind of shit?"

"Nation State actors," Mac answered. "Not ours, but some nation-state clown show out there has them. North Korea, Iran, China… I'm betting Chinese tech."

The wind kicked up as they spoke, clearing the air to the point is was breathable again and extending visibility.

"Commie bastards… that's who it is," Falcone growled like a she-bear that just spotted a tourist encroaching on her cub's personal space.

"It might be radical Islamic extremists… but I'm betting China."

"Assholes."

"Total assholes. They don't want us getting our mitts on that maggot Berkley Bartson and making him talk," Mac surmised.

"There isn't much left to get, Mac… this place is a parking lot."

"We need aerial support. We'll never find them on a foot patrol."

"He has to be dead. What makes you think he's alive?" Erika waved her hand toward the blast scene, supporting her question.

"These kinds of people are experts at letting everyone else suffer while they get away. It's almost their trademark. He had to have some kind of exit strategy. What would you do if you had unlimited money?"

Falcone thought about it for a second. "I have a friend in Arizona who dug tunnels everywhere under his place… I'll go with tunnels."

"If they got a heads up, he rabbited."

Mac called Deeter. Within minutes their extraction ride came overhead and checked the area with the FLIR.

A tinny voice responded. "The blast radius is FUBAR for a mile. There is a heat signature indicating somebody is working their way down the south valley trail. They're two miles ahead of you."

"Pick us up. I want to be put down two miles ahead of them."

"Copy that."

Mac turned his attention back to Erika. "Ready to get some information out of this worm?"

She smiled, "Oh yeah."

## The White House – Oval Office

From behind the Resolute Desk, the President ordered a cheeseburger and a diet soda for a working lunch in his private office. He ordered a salad for his daughter and a pork chop plate for his son. It was time for an update on the virus emergency. Ten minutes later they were in the private office discussing Mac's progress.

"Blew that son of a bitch up, huh?" The President asked on being briefed about the plantation bomb.

"Yes, sir. It looks like the Chinese dropped a big assed bomb on it." Deeter answered.

The President said, "China," in his odd way of pronouncing it when he was emphasizing the word.

The President's daughter added, "It looks like our people are in pursuit of that scumbag Berkley Bartson now… It appears his security detail might have gotten him out before the explosion. We can watch it in real time from if you wish."

The President responded enthusiastically. "Hey, I'd like to watch something besides fake news. Let's watch Mac and Falcone work. I'd love it."

The First Daughter picked up a remote and quickly linked a satellite feed from her phone to a television mounted on the wall.

An overhead shot that appeared to be taken from a rising helicopter depicted two commandos being deployed into small clearing in a jungle-like environment.

"That's called *hot roping*, sir," Deeter explained as the pair slid down a rope from the helicopter to the ground.

"That's some tough customers. You're not going to find anyone tougher. That, I can tell you. It's true. I think everyone would agree," the President responded with boyish enthusiasm for his special operatives. "They're like our police and military. The absolute best."

As the helicopter gained more altitude the camera revealed that the pair was about eight hundred yards ahead of a small group of men descending a narrow trail into a deep valley.

"I have a feeling we will be getting the location of the secret bioweapon lab very soon, sir," The First Son commented.

The President agreed. "I think they're gonna knock the hell out of these guys."

## JUNGLE OUTSIDE OF CHIANG RAI, THAILAND

Mac and Falcone hit the ground running, sprinting towards the trail to set up the ambush of the treasonous tech guru and his security detail. They received live updates in their ear comms from the helicopter pilot. Mac quickly spotted the ground he liked for their next move.

"Take up a concealed position here," Mac whispered breathlessly as they hunkered down to finalize the plan. "Let them move past you. Up ahead will be the ambush point. I'll engage them and push them back towards you. They'll keep the target as far as possible from me as they can while they back up, so you should be able to separate him from the survivors of my attack. The trick will be to get the target alive. Try not to kill him."

"Shit happens, pal."

"I know. I'm the poster child for shit happens. But just let them get past you. We'll box them in and take the security team down hard."

"Copy that."

Falcone had the AK47 she retrieved from a body earlier, her knives, and her 1911 with her, but she wished she still had the M4. It was her favorite and much more accurate at longer ranges, at least for her.

Falcone took up the position on the south side of the trail. Mac moved further down to initiate the encounter from a narrow rocky spot on the north side of the trail ahead of the group.

Mac spotted their point man. He was too far extended for providing cover in this situation, perhaps three hundred yards in front of the others which, in the jungle, is too far for a protective operation with only five guys.

As the point man reached him, Mac stepped out from behind a tree and hammer-fisted him on the head then lifted him off the ground with a brutal uppercut punch. The man collapsed in a heap. Mac stomped his head flat, finishing the job.

He dragged the body into the brush and kicked some leaves and dirt around the area covering up the bloody brain stuff that remained on the trail. He quietly wiped his sticky boot off on some moss and went back to watch mode.

A minute later four security men came down the trail with a goofy looking bastard sporting a Nickelback T-shirt, plaid shorts, crocks, and a red cotton beanie pulled over his ears. He was at least in his late forties, making his outfit look that much stupider. He *had* to be the target.

Mac stepped out again and shot the first two men in the detail. As expected, the last two surviving security men dragged their protectee back up the trail at a dead run.

Falcone was ready. She flipped down the bayonet on the AK, spearing the first guy, kicking the nerd in the nuts, and shooting the last of the three men in the chest. Mac was with her before the target could quick puking up his lunch.

*Getting your balls smashed will do that*, Mac thought as he examined the scene.

"Hey, I didn't kill him," Falcone said a bit defensively.

"No worries. He'll be able to talk soon."

Li Wei regained a moment of consciousness. *Dammit,* he thought… *I've been killed. An amateur move watching behind me instead of looking ahead. And that bitch stabbed me in the guts…* The security operative didn't see his life before his eyes or a white light. Instead he saw a beautiful woman and the huge man dragging his protectee down the trail by his ankles. He could hear a helicopter circling. Then he sucked down his last breath and bled out.

# Chapter 12 - Never piss off an American with a gun

Back aboard the helicopter and on the way out of Thailand, the pilot communicated with Mac via the intercom. "We have the range to get over the Andaman Sea... there is a freighter there we can land on and refuel. Where are we going from there?"

"Get me over the ocean and I'll let you know within ten minutes. Will that work?"

"Yes. We have a few hours... relax until then. I'll let you know when we are over the water."

"Copy that."

Mac looked at Erika who was busy wrapping duct tape around their prisoner, tightening him up like a mummy.

The man had a large lump by his temple where Erika clocked him after a rude comment about her boobs.

"He should have kept his mouth shut," Mac commented.

"Well, I can take jokes and shit from my friends. And I can totally dish it out too. But this little pervert needed a lesson in appropriate behavior around strangers… and did you see his t-shirt? I should shoot him just for that shit."

Mac didn't pick up on what he said on the trail to get knocked the fuck out, but it must have been bad. And what kind of asshole gets smart with someone he just saw murder people with a bayonet. Stupid Silicon Valley assholes. "How long do you think he will be out?"

"Let him sleep until we're over the water. Then I can bring him around with smelling salts."

"Sounds good. I'm going to catch a nap. You can have a cold beer and take first watch on the prisoner."

"No problem."

Four hours later the pilot made an announcement, "Now approaching the Andaman Sea."

Erika retrieved smelling salts from the first aid kit and woke up their prisoner. "Rise and shine, maggot."

The billionaire tech genius stirred, "You can't do this to me. Do you know who I am?" He demanded after barely regaining consciousness.

"Yeah, we know who you are. And now we know your default personality is dickhead…"

He started to complain but caught a rabbit punch in his tender nuggets.

"This is amazing, Bartson. You're wrapped in duct tape and you're still an asshole," Mac commented. He looked at Falcone. "That makes this next part that much more precious."

250

Bartson interjected some panic. "What? Wait... What?"

Mac showed him the ice pick that he found in the wet bar. "We need to know where the bio-weapon lab is located."

"What lab?" he spouted off indignantly.

Mac stabbed Bartson through his cheeks with the ice pick. "I know this makes it harder to talk, but I want you to know I don't like you and bad shit will happen if you piss me off."

Berkley Bartson made a funny noise with his tongue as it flipped back and forth over the ice pick jammed through his mouth between his teeth, making him look like a shish kabobbed appetizer. His beady little eyes darted back and forth like he couldn't believe this was real.

Falcone suppressed a snicker. *Good times*, she thought.

"When you spoke, you sounded like you had an accent," Mac commented as he pulled the ice pick out of Berkley, giving him a moment of reprieve to talk.

Berkeley spit up a little blood before speaking, "I'm originally from the UK... I have dual citizenship."

Mac frowned, "I hate dual citizenship." He stabbed Bartson in the arm with the ice pick causing the prisoner to make a yipping sound.

"Oww.... I'm mainly an American," Bartson offered desperately.

"Kind of a piss poor American, if you ask me," a semi-disinterested Falcone added to the discussion as she ran a file over her fingernails.

Mac stopped his interrogation to ask, "Where the hell did you get a fingernail file?"

"I always carry one. Doing this kind of shit is hard on a manicure."

He returned his attention to the prisoner. "So... I still need to know where the bio-lab is... and you're going to tell me... or I start doing mean shit to you."

"What? Mean? No, no, no... I'll cooperate. No mean shit... please!"

"Where is it!"

"I don't know."

Mac stabbed him in the wiener.

Bartson screamed. Then he found that he couldn't stop talking.

"It's in Baja... East of a village called San Antonio Dis las Minas in the desert hills. It's a series of block buildings in sort of a hexagon like a fort. You can't miss it. I never liked those guys. I had no idea this shit was going on. I'm like on your side, really."

"Are you sure? Because, I don't want to have to do this kind of shit." Mac stabbed him in the leg.

Bartson squealed, "No... I'm sure... I helped design it. I've been there. It's there. I promise."

Mac was satisfied. "This little commie is all yours, Falcone."

Bartson objected, "I'm not a communist."

McCartney pulled the ice pick out of his leg. "This lady thinks you *are* a communist... so... take it up with her."

"Yeah, take it up with me you little commie prick."

Mac touched the intercom button. "Take it to eight hundred feet. That should do it.

Instantly the passengers felt the sense of dropping as Mac opened the sliding hatch mid-ship of the helicopter.

"What are you doing?' Bartson cried.

Falcone answered. "Feeding fish, asshole. I thought all you environmentalists hated people and loved nature... Circle of life bitch." She stood him up, put a boot to his ass, and launched him out the door.

McCartney secured the hatch and touched the intercom button again. "Let the logistics crew know we're headed for Baja."

Falcone got up from her seat, "Want a beer?" She asked as she pulled a cold Butt Whisker beer out of the refrigerator.

"Does Dolly Parton sleep on her back? Mac responded rhetorically.

She grabbed a second beer and handed it to McCartney. She took a long pull on her beer and said, "Let me be really honest with you here, Mac. I don't think I'll miss that little maggot."

"Me neither," Mac said as he took a sip of beer. "He was annoying."

"Totally."

Mac chugged the rest of the bottle and retrieved another one for himself and another for Falcone as he moved toward the secure office in the back of the helicopter. "I got to call the boss."

Erika took the beer. "I'm going to finish this and grab a catnap. And tell the boss we're going to need more guns. A shit ton of guns."

## THE GREAT HALL OF THE PEOPLE - BEIJING

Zhao went berserk in his private office quarters. *How could someone get so many forces in place so quickly? How could they locate and capture Bartson with such ease? Ridiculous.* And now the lab was in play and the weapon wouldn't be ready to be deployed for over a day and a half. This series of setbacks could collapse the entire operation. It would certainly end the technological advantage Zhao brought to China with stolen American technology and intellectual property.

*I need men on the scene in Baja... All of them,* he thought as he reached a near panic state. Even the President of China had no idea what he had been up to. Zhao expected to complete his plan, announce it to the world, and in response to overwhelming gratitude he expected to be given the President's job and be made Chairman of the Communist Party by unanimous consent. Now the plan was at severe risk. *I could be executed.* Zhao ran to the bathroom and puked.

## Bio-Weapon Lab - Baja California

"Something happened at the Tea Plantation," the Executive Director announced grimly to the eight men and women sitting around the conference table.

"What was it, what happened," an older woman in a lab coat asked.

An agitated young man, perhaps in his late twenties jumped up from his seat and interjected, "They got blown the fuck up, that's what happened. And my boss is dead as shit!"

The Executive Director half-heartedly attempted to calm him. It wasn't easy. He was on the verge of panic himself. Things weren't good. But they had to keep it together or the shit would hit the fan. "We don't know for sure he's dead. He's missing at this point. Let's all remain calm."

The panicking young scientist wasn't done. "Fuck calm. Any minute a bunch of special forces guys are going to nuke us, or shoot us, or torture us… I don't know… Bad stuff! I'm out of here." The man jumped out of his seat and headed for the door. At the same moment the head of security came into the conference room. The young man ran face first into his stomach and bounced back on the floor landing on his ass.

The security head was monstrous in size and demeanor. He wore a black jump suit with a leather gun belt and a black ball cap. He had a thick jagged scar running from his chin to his left ear. At six foot eight and three hundred and twenty pounds, he wasn't merely large. He was a frightening beast of a human being... if he was *even* human.

The massive man seemed unfazed by the impact. He reached down and grabbed the younger man by the throat, lifting him off the ground at arm's length and threw him back in his chair.

"We are not panicking. This is under control. It would be best if you don't make me kill you." His words were guttural and choppy. His voice had the tenor of someone who seldom speaks.

The Executive Director reiterated the man's words, "Yes, no panicking. Nothing is going to happen. Don't make him kill you... or me. Please..."

The security man ignored the pleading director and continued, "There is no need for concern. I am bringing in extra security forces. They will be here soon, and we can continue with the work as normal. So, I must insist... finish your jobs... work as though your life depended on completing this mission."

His words carried the stench of threats. The message was clear. Complete the job or die where you stand.

## CORPORATE JET – OVER THE PACIFIC OCEAN

Deeter grinned as he issued weapons to the two corporate fixers. It made him feel like Santa Clause. "Mac, I have something special for you. I'd love to hear how it works in action."

"What do you have?" Mac gave him his full attention.

Mac handed him a belt fed machine gun. "It's a Sig MG 338 Light machine gun in .338 Norma Magnum. It bites somewhere between an AK and a fifty. Perfect for doing cool stuff."

"Well, doing cool stuff is in our job description," Mac acknowledged.

Erika was enjoying herself and was anxious to get in on the fun. "What do you have for me? I prefer old school, you know. But I'll be open minded."

"Try this," Deeter retrieved a black canvas bag that looked like it held a tennis racket.

"I don't play Tennis… I don't even like Tennis… except for that Rick Macci dude… He's a stud.

"Who?" Despite his upbringing, Deeter was more of an outdoorsman than a tennis club guy.

Erika didn't feel like explaining. "Never mind. Let's see what you have." She opened the bag and found a Patriot Rogue .308 Light Weight pistol. Erika was impressed. "Ohhh… I like."

Deeter elaborated. It's a lightweight AR10 that chambers 308 and has a twelve-inch barrel give or take a half an inch. It's designed to reduce recoil and enhance accuracy. I have two of them for you."

"Nice…"

"And, of course, a pair of 1911s."

"Duh." She gave Deeter a sisterly elbow in the ribs.

"What's our transportation when we get there?" Mac inquired.

"I have something special. Do you know that 1977 El Camino that Gerry Derrickson built?"

"Yeah… the King of the Hammers rig?"

"Yeah… I commissioned him to build two clones. One for my garage and one for you on this mission."

"Whoa!"

"Exactly!" Deeter assumed a demonic grin. "But that's not all."

"What… there's more?"

Erika put her hand up. "No disrespect, sir… but you two knobs sound like a damned television game show. I'm not a gearhead… what the hell are you talking about?"

Mac answered excitedly. "Imagine an old El Camino that is licensed to kill with 31-inch mud terrain tires, four-wheel drive capabilities that are crazy ridiculous, and a transmission that is wanted for murder in fourteen states... that's what we're talking about."

"Well, I am an American, so obviously I know what King of the Hammers is, but I'll take your word on the rest... so, what is the rest of the story... you said there was more?" Erika asked.

"Besides being custom fitted for comfort and elegance by our family's personal car-makers it has something very special I think you both will like."

Erika interrupted. "Did you say personal car-makers?"

Deeter shrugged as if she asked him if he could recommend a good barber, "Mostly they just customize luxury or rare cars for us, but it keeps the team busy full time. It's a matter of thrift. For example, rather than buying the original Bullit Mustang for thirty million or more, I had them manufacture a clone for just eight million. No matter how much you have, if you count the pennies the dollars will follow."

Falcone blinked once and gave Mac an empty *mind-blown* stare.

Mac waved her off and whispered, "There are people on this planet that have wealth we can't comprehend. Just learn from them and don't make a big deal about it."

Deeter enthusiastically continued ignoring the back chatter, "But here is what's cool." He pulled an

8.5x11 photo out of a leather folder. The El Camino has a Dillon Aero fifty caliber Gatling gun mounted in the bed. It will crank out fifteen hundred rounds of fifty caliber BMG at about fifteen hundred rounds per minute."

Mac took the photo of the car and gun combo. "I've read about these. This is that triple barrel rig… It does about twenty-five rounds a second, right?"

Deeter smiled slyly. "Afraid so."

"That ought to light somebody's ass up!" Mac said with awe.

Falcone jumped into the conversation again, "From now on I'll just go ahead and get paid in these instead of money if that's okay."

Deeter pursed his lips taking the request seriously before answering with the bad news. "I anticipated you would say that, so I looked into it. They can't manufacture them fast enough to keep up with payroll, so we'll have to stick with money for now. But if you want one for yourself, we have a few spares in inventory. I can give you one. Call it a bonus."

Erika let out an uncharacteristically gleeful giggle. "I love my job."

Deeter continued with the briefing. "We also have an array of handguns, shotguns, and rifles waiting for you chosen on the preferences you've previously established. Everything is waiting for you on an eighteen-wheeler about forty miles from the target. But now we need to look at the job. There is a bio-weapon plant in Baja. It has about one hundred top-tier security people and about twenty-five scientists. We want you to go there, kill everybody, and then confirm the weapon is on site. Once you give us the confirmation, we'll hit it with a missile from outer space."

"How long will we have to get out of there?"

"Oh, maybe twenty minutes."

"What's the blast radius?"

"I'd say, thirty miles."

"The terrain?"

"Standard Baja shit show of desert, rocks, and small mountains."

"That doesn't give us much leeway."

Deeter answered like a used-car dealer explaining how warranty doesn't cover your problem, "Yeah... I think you'll need to go really fast."

"I'm not loving this part." Falcone said sarcastically in a sing-song voice.

Deeter pressed on, "Did I mention that the El Camino has the same ballistic glass that the President's limo uses... and the cab is lined with level three Kevlar?"

"Sounding better as an escape vehicle already."

"It's like a bomb shelter on wheels… very big wheels. If you can even get ten miles away from ground zero, park this behind cover, and get in the cab there is a fifty-fifty chance you won't get blown up that much."

"Cover?" Mac asked.

"I recommend parking behind a mountain."

Mac replied fatalistically, "When you put it that way, it sounds almost too easy."

"So, we're a go?" Deeter asked.

"Not a problem," Falcone interjected. "We'll knock this out and be back in San Diego before the fuckers know what hit them."

# Chapter 13 - Never piss off McCartney and Falcone with a gun

BAJA, MEXICO

The helicopter dropped Mac and Falcone near the tractor trailer rig right containing their equipment. The pair walked to the truck and encountered a balding gray-haired old man sporting a yellow aloha shirt, flip flops, cargo shorts, and a cowboy hat waiting for them. He had a tanker style holster slung over his chest with what looked like a Sig 220 strapped in it. But he didn't seem like an immediate threat to them.

"You are?" Mac asked cautiously.

"Just call me Lynch," the old man in the Hawaiian shirt answered with a pleasant smile. "I'll be your delivery man today." He extended his right.

As Mac shook hands with him, he noticed the old timer had the scarred knuckles of an old school karate man.

Falcone shook hands next and responded with a mix of courtesy and curiosity, "So what do you have for us today, Mr. Lynch?"

He answered her with a mischievous wink rather than words. The old-timer ambled over to the truck and pushed a red button on the side of the truck that automatically opened the back loading door and dropped a steel ramp. He ambled up into the trailer.

Mac and Falcone looked at each other, shrugged, and then followed him to check out the cargo. Inside the truck was the El Camino as promised and crates of weapons, ammo, and equipment. *Is it my birthday*, Mac asked himself as he examined the bounty of war tools.

Lynch chuckled at the expressions of awe on the faces of Mac and Erika., "Why, if I was ten years younger, I'd go with you on whatever it is you're going to go do with this stuff."

"You're still welcome to tag along, sir." Mac said with respect and gentility. Being raised in the South, Mac was inclined to show respect to his elders, even if they were driving around in a foreign country with a truck load of illegal weapons.

The old man looked genuinely disappointed as he declined the offer. "Not this trip, unfortunately. I have some folks like you up in Alaska waiting for me to bring them a load of special toys… not this cool, but sort of like this. The delivery company I work for keeps me pretty busy since I retired."

"Retired from what?" Erika asked, expecting him to describe some military or police agency.

"Let's just say *retired* and leave it at that," the old man said cryptically. "The best friendships have a foundation of privacy."

Falcone knuckle bumped with him with a knowing grin. "Yeah, let's just say that."

Erika pointed to back of the rig at another off-road vehicle. "Is that for us too?"

"No… that one is a for a different assignment," he answered vaguely.

"Fair enough."

They unloaded their equipment and bid farewell to the old codger as he climbed into the cab, tipped his hat, and drove down the dirt road, disappearing in a dust cloud.

## THE WHITE HOUSE - WASHINGTON DC

The President of the United States initiated a phone call with the Director of the CIA.

Clammer took the call. "Yes Mr. President," Clammer stammered out, nervous as a flasher at a weeny roast.

"Mr. Director, I'm having a meeting with the Attorney General tomorrow here at the Oval Office. I'd appreciate it if you could attend. It is regarding a matter of some urgency, you know, counterintelligence, spies, traitors… that sort of thing. We can't really hold the meeting without your presence. I'll send government limos for you both at two next Tuesday afternoon."

"Of course, sir. I'll be there."

The President abruptly disconnected.

Clammer threw up in his wastebasket.


In the White House, the President, Vice-President, and the Attorney General were gathered around the Resolute Desk laughing their asses off.

The typically stoic Vice-President was uncharacteristically mirthful. "Now do the FBI Director!"

## BAJA, MEXICO

"So, what's the plan?" Falcone asked.

"When we get closer, you drive, and I'll man the gun. We roll up and kill everybody."

"Sounds good."

Using the integrated GPS system in the El Camino they approached the final canyon they needed to cross before dropping into the valley where the lab was located. They parked behind the mountain peak.

"This might be our fallback position."

"It's only eight miles from ground zero." Erika said with some concern in her voice.

"Yeah but they always double these blast radius estimates… I'm sure we'd be fine at even five miles.".

"Are you sure? I've never heard that before."

"Pretty sure, Falcone. I think I saw it on the Science Channel."

"Yeah, fine. I don't give a shit… If I'm going to go out, I want to go out behind the wheel of this bad boy anyway."

"Copy that.

Both operatives stepped out of the vehicle and put on their ultra-thin level five armor created by DARPA and their ballistic helmets with integrated drop down enhanced virtual reality goggles and comm units.

Mac climbed into the bed, strapping into the safety harness and Erika hopped in behind the wheel.

She revved the engine twice then hit it.

They emerged from behind the small mountain and almost flew down a winding trail, missing most of the switchbacks, rolling downhill and balls out over the rocky terrain crushing everything in their path at a bruising fifty miles an hour.

Mac bounced around the bed like a tennis ball in a laundry dryer.

They quickly closed the gap on the lab compound and found a smoother access road. She kicked it up to seventy as they moved within a half a mile of the facility.

## COVERT BIOWEAPONS LAB SECURITY OFFICE — BAJA, MEXICO

"Mr. Kilborn… we have vehicular activity on the perimeter," the skinny man in the black jump suit announced from his desk facing a series of flat panel screens.

The Director of Security gave the monitoring officer his full attention, "What does it look like? How many?"

"I think it's just one vehicle… it appears to be some four-wheeler types. It's probably nothing."

"No… unlikely. This is no coincidence. It's a raid. Notify the perimeter security teams and initiate a lockdown protocol. Sound the alarm."

"For one car?"

Kilborn slapped the man hard enough to knock him out of his chair. "Follow orders… I have no interest in your musings."

The man picked himself off of the floor and started hitting buttons on his console like Liberace banging piano keys.

An audible alert tone reminiscent of a World War Two air raid warning siren began to wail across the desert like an angry cat being dragged by the tail.

Kilborn retrieved his AK47 from his office. He also grabbed his fighting knife and slid it into the sheath on his belt. He took one more look at the computer screens and then left the building to investigate the intrusion.

## BIOWEAPON LAB PERIMETER – BAJA, MEXICO

Mac was able to stabilize himself more effectively when the El Camino hit the graded access road. He went to full Rat Patrol mode and swung the fifty caliber Gatling gun towards the first group of security people he saw.

Maybe ten men were moving in a loose group, guns at the ready, and approaching the El Camino's path.

Mac estimated range. One short three second burst of fire disintegrated that threat. They weren't even a skid mark in the shorts of Mexico anymore.

Falcone turned hard right and smashed through the gate into the interior of the compound, leaving most of the perimeter responders outside the facility playing catch-up.

Kilborn saw the breach and cursed, "Assholes… nobody hits a place this fast. Reckless bastards!" He ran towards the main lab facility to rally a stand if necessary.

Mac ripped another burst at the closest building, opening a masonry block exterior wall like a ball peen hammer to a balsa wood box. He pulled a 40MM grenade launcher out of his coat and fired one round of HE into the hole.

Men and machines stirred dirt, dust, and chaos as a dozen combat ready dune buggies skidded into the compound transporting heavily armed security personnel into the fray. The first four vehicles to appear from an underground garage met the wrath of the Gatling gun. A ten second burst of fifty caliber took them out of the fight. The other eight vehicles moved towards a structure that was partially underground and set up a defensive perimeter.

As he spotted targets, Mac continued to fire the Gatling gun interspersed with deploying grenades from his old M79 launcher, destroying buildings and killing people. So far, the mission was a success. Most of the security team was obliterated within ten minutes of the first shot being fired. It was almost time to start doing entries and checking the interiors for the virus. Just that one underground building to take down. Then things suddenly got intense.

## CIA HEADQUARTERS - LANGLEY, VIRGINIA

Clammer dialed the FBI Director in a panic.

"What is it, Clam Man?"

Clammer was too freaked to bristle at the offensive nickname. "The President is looking for us. We're screwed."

"Shit."

"We need to bail."

"Can we call China?"

"They hate us too."

"The tech guys?"

"Mostly dead."

"Shit."

"I know."

"How long do we have?"

"Days… less than a week."

"Every man for himself, Clammer. I'm out of here."

Clammer disconnected. *I wonder if I can cut a deal with POTUS and rat that asshole out?* he thought. He immediately reconsidered, *screw it, I'm out of here.*

At the FBI headquarters, the Director was mentally speculating about his situation, *I wonder if I can arrange some sort of a deal with the President and give up that little weasel bastard?* He thought about the downside, considered the millions in payoff money he had stashed, and made a change of plans. *No way… I'm making a run for it. I'll be gone in a week.*

## COVERT BIOWEAPONS LAB – BAJA, MEXICO

Bodies were strewn across the facility as the precision mortar fire rained hell down on the compound. Erika swerved and serpentine to avoid being targeted but there wasn't enough room to operate. And now the men in the eight remaining dune buggies were coordinating fire on them too. *Where the hell is that mortar fire coming from?*

Mac decided that the underground building had to be the lab location. He poured fire back at the eight dune buggy crews as best he could with the onslaught of incoming rounds heading his way. He yelled at Erika, "Get back... We have to find some cover and figure out a way past those guys."

"Copy that."


"On a mountain top almost a mile away, an old man in a Hawaiian shirt and cowboy hat took careful aim with his Barret 50. Spotting the mortar was easy. They weren't that careful. They thought there were only two people involved in this little gig. The bad guys didn't calculate Falcone and Mac might have a guardian angel.

Lynch carefully pressed the trigger and fired one round. It hit one of the mortar crew members in the side and spread him across the slope.

Round two hit the ammo. The explosion was memorable. The mortar and crew were dead.

Lynch lit a Lucky Strike and relaxed for a moment. "You have to enjoy the little things in life. I'm grateful for every day." He had gotten a bit philosophical in is old age.


Falcone saw a flash on the hillside as the mortar team vaporized. She smiled, *thanks Lynch.* Erika spun the wheel hard and spoke to Mac on the comm unit. "The mortar is down. Let's rush these bastards."

"Copy that."

Erika gunned it and the El Camino lurched into the off-road world's version of warp factor nine. The engine roared in tandem with the Gatling gun as they ran directly into the line of eight buggies.

"Hold on!" Erika yelled.

She stomped on the gas and drove over the dune buggies crushing the desert vehicles flat and killing about a third of the remaining security force. She pulled out her semi-auto sawed off shotgun and started smoking maggots. Anybody that moved got a load of buckshot. She hopped out and went to the handguns. She blazed away with the matched pair of Valor 45s, dropping targets as she moved. Each 240-grain jacketed hollow point causing massive destruction. Her aggression confounded the security teams as they lost unit cohesion and began running.

Mac kept the pressure on the security people with the Gatling gun until he burned through the last of the ammo. He switched to a Custom M4, bailed out of the bed of the El Camino, and started terminating threats.

Falcone and McCartney gained momentum and started rolling back the defenders. Mac noticed a large man, almost his size, run to a steel hatch on the side of the underground building and secure himself inside. Mac gave Falcone a hand signal indicating he was going after the big man but was interrupted by some asshole kung fu dude executing a flying side kick into the back of his head.

Mac tumbled forward stunned. *Where did that little prick come from?* He touched his ear comm, "Falcone, get that big turd who ran inside the building. I got somebody here who needs their ass beat."

"Copy."

Falcone sprinted to the entrance, placed a breeching charge against it, and blew the steel door off the wall and part of the wall with it.

"Whoopsie." *No such thing as too much explosive material.*

She made a tactical entry in pursuit of the big guy. Erika sensed something familiar about the man. She sprinted down a series of steel stairs. At three floors down she saw stars. Somebody sucker punched her with a gigantic fist out of nowhere. Erika fell flat on her ass, stunned and disoriented. Her combat acumen switched to autopilot. Her response was spontaneous and effective. Not being a fair fighter by nature anyway, she unslung her shotgun and poured a wall of lead down the stairway. "Back off, asshole!"

A voice further down the stairwell cried out in pain.

*I guess I got somebody. I hope it was a bad guy.*

Falcone reloaded the shotgun and continued down more cautiously this time. Her head was still ringing from the blow. *Son of a bitch must pay,* she thought, mentally quoting the hero of her favorite movie.

Erika made her way to the bottom floor, maybe five stories down. She spotted a man throwing switches and doing stuff that looked nefarious as hell. *Oh hell no… he's going to deploy the weapon.*

Erica took a shot at the big man with her shotgun causing him to stumble forward a bit, but he continued working.

*What the hell?*

She scampered across the large lab room over tables and benches, sprinting towards him, firing as she ran.

He turned as she closed and fired at her with a handgun, hitting her square in the ceramic plate over her sternum.

"Shit!"

She felt that one. Large bore handgun bullets hurt even with bullet proof protection.

Erika emptied the shotgun again hitting him and driving him back against the floor to ceiling panels of switches and monitors.

He returned fire without effect.

Then she recognized him. This was the guy who she carved up in Belarus in a knife fight. He was a bad ass and she got lucky that day.

"How about a rematch, Spanky?"

The insult went over his head. "My name is not Spanky. I am Kilborn… and I now I will have the pleasure of taking your life."

"Bring it, pussy."

Kilborn pushed a table out of his way, pulled his battle knife and closed the gap with the much smaller Falcone.

Falcone was starting to doubt her initial bravado. *Did this piece of shit grow or something? I don't remember him being that fucking big.* The Ka Bars came out. "Let's dance, pretty boy!"

He launched the first attack using a low swipe with his ten-inch blade Citadel Tanto.

Falcone side stepped it and slashed upward, cutting off a chunk of his nose.

Kilborn squealed as blood ran down his face.

"Did that hurt?" she asked as she circled him in a low combat stance.

Enraged he lunged again, sticking her in the shoulder but not too deeply. Falcone ignored the wound. She countered with a snap kick to the nuts, reversing to a low floor level spin sweeping kick. She caught him behind the ankles and dropped the big man on his back.

She raised her knife for the coup de grace.

Boom! A blinding flash and smell of gun smoke.

Mac smiled with the smoking 454 Casul in his hand. "Sorry, were you killing this guy or what?"

At first Falcone was a little indignant. "Yes... I was killing this guy until you so rudely interrupted and blew his head off for no reason.

"I had a reason."

"What?"

"We're in a hurry. That's the reason. This is the lab. I'm guessing those vats over there with skeleton heads painted on them are the bad scary shit, and we killed all the bad guys. Time to call in an air strike."

"When did you become Mr. Responsibility?" Erika asked with a shit eating grin.

"I've always been able to be responsible, I just never had to be the responsible guy before… so… wanna blow this shit hole up?"

"Hell yeah!"

The operators ran to the El Camino and hopped in the cab. Erika drove while Mac signaled confirmation for the depleted uranium rod to be dropped from space into the complex. There would be no radiation, no one could prove where it came from, and there would be no evidence left as to what it was. The only thing left in the aftermath would be a crater.

Falcone tried to retrace their route torturing the El Camino into extreme performance. The bounced up the hills on the massive tires until they reached their planned hiding place to await the blast.

Falcone put it in park, secured the emergency brake, and said, "Just to be on the safe side, strap in."

They both secured the five-point racing harnesses and tightened their helmets. Then they assumed crash position.

Mac sort of expected a whistling sound or something like that preceding the blast as the projectile entered the atmosphere, but there was only silence… until there wasn't.

The blast was unlike anything they had ever experienced. The El Camino was thrown into the far hillside tumbling down into the rocky valley below. The cloud of dust enveloped them making the Thailand bomb seem like a firecracker. The car came to rest upside down in the rocky debris.

Minutes later, when the ground stopped shaking, Erika stated, "I'm tired of getting blown up."

Mac agreed. "Yeah… me too."

"And I think the indestructible car got destructed."

"No shit."

"What do we do?"

"Start walking."

The extricated themselves from the wreckage and made their way west. When they got to the road two hours later a familiar truck came by.

"You two need a ride?"

"Yeah, Lynch… I think we could use a ride. Drop us off at the border if you don't mind."

"Hop in and grab a beer out of the cooler in the back. I'll get you're there before dark."

"Copy that."

They rode in silence for fifteen minutes sipping beer.

Lynch broke the hush and asked, "Did you get them all?"

Mac answered, "Yeah. We got them. Every last rat bastard they had."

# Chapter 14 - Never piss off a man of violence with a gun

## SURFSIDE ESTATE - CORONADO, CALIFORNIA

Mac and Falcone enjoyed a margarita while Deeter sipped a diet soda.

"Dad is ecstatic. Seriously, this lifted an enormous burden off his shoulders. And despite the uh, unfortunate body count, you kept the true significance of this mission secret. As far as anyone knows, this whole thing was some vague international crime syndicate sorting out a territorial conflict. You know, communists, dictators, oligarchs… the usual assholes who do nefarious shit. The United States retains absolute deniability."

"Well, that's good, I guess," Mac said, not being remotely interested in government workings, business, or boards of directors.

"And… he is giving you each a paid month of vacation."

Erika smiled at the news, "I can live with that. I had a knife fighting competition in Bogota I wanted to go too. Can my fiancée go with me? He's between jobs. We might just make an extended vacation out of it."

The confused expression on Deeter's face was tinged with a slight hint of fear at the implications of having a total maniac in the President's service. "Your vacation is a *knife fight*?"

Mac answered with a conspiratorial stage whisper, "Chill Deeter, she relaxes by slicing up assholes with a Ka Bar. She's a Marine... you know how they get."

Deeter laughed. "What about you, Mac?"

"I got one more thing to do, then I'm coming back here to spend my break doing happy hours, watching bikinis, and enjoying sunsets on the beach."

Falcone frowned. She understood the grave implications of what McCartney so casually mentioned. "Will you be needing some help with that *one more thing*?"

Mac smiled, "No. This is something I will need to take care of alone."

Falcone nodded perspicaciously... *Payback for Pearson. I think someone will finally see that primary weapon the old man bitched so much about, and when see it, I don't think they are going to be happy,* she thought.

## SHAN STATE - MYANMAR

Sleep eluded Colonel Ko. His sprawling estate in the jungles of Myanmar felt empty and cold. He needed a drink. He touched the intercom button on the nightstand intending to order his personal chef to send up a Single malt scotch on the rocks and some shrimp.

Nothing.

He tried to turn on a lamp, but the power was out.

"Idiots!" Someone must have failed to fuel the generator again.

Per his habit, he slid a throwing knife into the back of the waistband of his boxer shorts and wandered downstairs… Something was amiss. *The servants aren't responding…Where the hell is my security force?* Ko realized he was alone in the house.

He strode out of the gloom of the mansion into the outer courtyard where at least he would have the benefit of starlight.

A shimmer of movement in the shadows… *I am not alone.*

A man… a giant man stood partially concealed within the dark walls, arms at his sides and relaxed in his posture, one foot placed inches ahead of the other and his body almost imperceptibly angled. His posture did not reflect a combat stance but was instead detached and non-aggressive. *What does he want? Who dares enter my home?*

For an extended moment, the two men exchanged ice cold stares. Finally, the intruder spoke.

"You killed my partner, Ko." Mac's voice tightened, forcing himself to utter the words rather than murder Ko immediately. "He was my friend."

*An American,* Ko surmised after hearing his words. "So, you found me. And you believe you will exact vengeance?" Ko now knew precisely who this trespasser was. The time had come. An accounting for the American called Pearson's death.

Mac replied. "It looks that way doesn't it. Who hired you to take down the estate at Lake Tekapo?"

His circumstances puzzled Ko. *How was I possibly found here? This shouldn't be happening,* he thought. *How did this brute discover the whereabouts of my home… a fortress-like compound built deep in the jungles of the most remote and dangerous areas of Myanmar… a guarded secret known only to a few trusted men? No white man had ever even been there before, let alone an American.* He had to ask. "How? How could you know this location?"

Mac explained, "You're a jerk, Ko. People hate your guts. It wasn't hard to uncover a man willing to rat your miserable ass out."

"Impossible." Ko ruled his minions by fear. No one in his circle would dare give up information on him. This man had to be a nation-state actor with access to world-class intelligence capabilities.

Ko couldn't make out any details of the man's face beyond it being obscured with a thick unkempt beard and long black hair, but he sensed Mac's disrespectful sneer at a visceral level.

Mac answered with casual contempt. "No… it's possible… your men are weak… like you. Now, who enlisted you to hit Tekapo?"

Ko saw no benefit in protecting the cowardly bureaucrat responsible for ordering Pearson's death. "Your infamous Director of the FBI is who requested that action."

The reply surprised Mac. "That sanctimonious pussy? Bullshit."

Ko elaborated. "It was him. We owed him for ordering the release of our Warlord's son from an American black site where he was being detained for human trafficking and international narcotics smuggling. Your Director didn't accept an offer of a cash payment. Instead he wanted to be owed a favor. Killing your man and everybody else on that miserable estate was the favor."

Mac frowned at the disconcerting information. "What a dick. Really?"

Ko snickered at the question. "Of course. These American officials protect each other while generating millions of dollars working for us. It's not that big of a secret."

"Any proof?"

"Look up who authorized the release of Bo Keng... He was being detained at a secluded location in the islands near the Bering Sea. The paper trail will confirm my words."

"I'll do that. Thanks. Sorry I can't return the favor and tell you which one of your people ratted you out. Now we have our own business to resolve."

"Rats? Ratting me out?" Ko grew weary of the conversation. Being held at gunpoint at his own home was an outrage. He became defiant. Ko killed for much less than this man's insolent chatter. Ko spit on the ground between them as he prepared to cope with his own imminent death. "Cowards...
pathetic cowards surround us. They are not men like you and me... If I must die, I wish to die at the hands of another man of violence. Do what you came here to do, bastard!" Ko stated proudly, as he thrust back his shoulders and assumed a position of attention.

Mac wasn't about to tolerate this macho shit show from his target. "Ko, you aren't a man of violence. You're just a man who acts out violently... a homicidal asshole. You and that worthless bunch of shit birds you call an army specialize in murdering people who are unarmed, outnumbered, or generally harmless. So, I don't know what to call you, a pussy, coward, dirtbag… but I do know you really need to go fuck yourself and die."

Ko pointed a finger at Mac as he countered with the most cutting insult he could devise. "You are mistaken. I am a man of violence. I've killed many men… all of them better than you… most of them better than your pathetic dead colleague." Ko smiled.

In the darkness, the unmitigated hate for Ko overwhelmed Mac's self-control. His loathing toward the man answerable for the death of his friend and mentor Pearson could no longer be repressed. He noticed a familiar itch in his trigger finger.

Ko perceived an opening. He snatched the blade out of his waistband and launched it underhanded at Mac with blistering speed.

The blade embedded into the meatiest part of Mac's right shoulder.

Mac didn't move. Unnerved by the lack of reaction, Ko sensed Mac might be impervious to the sharpened chunk of metal penetrating his skin and jutting out from his chest. *What kind of man is this?*

Mac looked disinterestedly at the wound, then slowly turned his attention to Ko. "Before I shove this knife up your ass, pal… Let's get something straight. You think you are a man of violence. So, I am guessing you need the answer to a question."

Ko stood slack jawed and confused. *What was this American scum talking about?* "A question?

What question?" Ko asked as his mind raced, searching for a move to make… any chance at all…he didn't see one except to run like hell if an opportunity to escape presented itself.

Mac continued. "Yeah … It's a simple question. How many."

Ko had nothing… *what is this riddle? What does he want?* With a state of confusion scrawled across his face Ko asked, "How many what?"

"How many men will it take to finally kill you."

Ko ignored Mac's words. Something new caught his attention… opportunity. Ko concealed any reaction to Mac as he watched four men from one of his roving security patrols moving like ghosts toward the open courtyard gates behind the big man. Ko liked the odds better now. The oafish American was so intent on talking that he was oblivious to their presence and soon… this filthy American dog will die. Ko stalled.

"So, American… How many men will it take to kill me? Ten? One hundred? One thousand?" He laughed as he taunted the soon to be deceased intruder.

"One, asshole. Just one."

Then things changed… they changed much faster than Ko expected.

Mac snapped his primary weapon out of the custom designed leather shoulder holster. Anyone with a shred of human decency might only describe the weapon Mac wielded as an object of terror, something awful. Something that should have never been created. It was evil incarnate, an instrument of the damned.

Only a man of Mac's size could conceal a ten-inch barrel semi-auto handgun with the gruesome power of one of the most savage big-game rifles in the world.

The unique design of the twelve-round magazine in the grip allowed holding the weapon in one hand if the gunman had the strength of a professional weightlifter. Mac kept the select-fire switch above the trigger on the fully automatic mode. Each of the massive .577 Tyrannosaurus rounds was a .585-inch diameter 750-grain projectile that would travel at almost twenty-five hundred feet per second while generating over ten thousand foot-pounds of kinetic energy.

While original intent of the .577 Tyrannosaurus was to drop the largest rhino on earth mid-charge at point-blank range, this ammunition design was brutal at a whole other level of horror. Each frangible bullet was engineered to be radically invasive, causing rapid exsanguination and ridiculous levels of organ damage to any living threat found on earth. Precision machined with multiple grooves, the bullets were made to break apart on impact and shred flesh like a meat grinder. The specially manufactured rounds, tipped with Mercury Fulminate and CS powder, were sealed with a thin coating of a custom solution, containing among other compounds, the fat of swine, a feature integrated for counter-terrorism initiatives.

It was insanity to believe that a man could fire such a devastating weapon without injury. But with the unique blow-back feature, and other classified elements created by a former Jet Propulsion Lab scientist, the recoil was manageable for a large man. The armorers, who's souls will likely burn in hell for creating this atrocity, only manufactured three of the guns. One of them was in Mac's hand.

Mac leveled the front sight of the hulking weapon at the big X-scar on Ko's forehead, the one put there years before by Erika Falcone. The perfect target for a perfect reckoning.

Ko's eyes widened in dread. *What maniac would have such a weapon?* Ko rarely experienced fear. He saw what was coming next and sensed the flow of warm urine running down his leg. A final humiliation.

Mac carefully pressed the trigger firing one round. The yellow and orange flames rolling out of the barrel extended far beyond the six-foot gap between the two men. Ko's head dissolved into what looked like a gallon jar of pizza sauce getting blasted out of a cannon. The rest of the bloodthirsty mercenary's body flew backward into a block wall as the spray of head goo painted it gray and red like wet stucco.

In one short fully automatic burst, Mac emptied the rest of the magazine into what remained of Ko, nearly disintegrating the man's body and leveling the block wall that the dead man had fallen against.

The primary weapon was now empty. Mac executed a forward shoulder roll and yanked his smaller every day carry gun, the Ruger 454 Casull, from the cross-draw belt holster.

Despite their extensive history of inflicting genocide and torture on helpless victims, Ko's security team stood stunned at the sight of the horrific murder, buying Mac a few seconds to reset and prepare for their imminent attempt at revenge.

As he moved, Ko's team recovered from the shock of Mac's initial blast, opening fire with their MP5 sub-machine guns. Mac was too big to find effective cover. He took two rounds, one in the butt and one across the fat of his belly.

*I'm fine*, he thought as he ducked behind a concrete statue of Buddha. He didn't feel fine but positive thinking is sometimes the only medical treatment available.

He came up firing, looking for head shots. He went left to right and scored a hit on target one, two, and three. Their heads exploded into mush as the thin red spray of death and dismemberment enveloped them. Target four suffered only a graze on the shoulder. The kinetic energy of the massive round still spun him across the courtyard and up against a tree four feet away. Mac walked up to him as he slid down the trunk and squirmed on the ground.

"Do you want to live?"

"Yes... let me go. I won't tell anyone what I saw here."

"Not today, asshole. You shot me in the butt, you rude little prick."

With the last round in the cylinder, Mac shot him in the face.

He reloaded both weapons before he turned and walked back to the body of Ko. Mac yanked the knife out of his shoulder, kicked over the glob of mush that was Ko's remains, making sure the remnants of his body were face down in the dirt, and shoved the throwing knife up his ass.

"That was for Pearson, you fucking maggot. See you in hell."

## GEORGETOWN - WASHINGTON DC

After ditching his security detail, The FBI Director bounded out of the elevator. The Chinese had arranged his private jet charter. Once aboard he would receive a briefcase full of money and diplomatic credentials in a new name, just like he had hoped for. In eight hours, he would be a wealthy man in a non-extradition country. *Fuck the President. Fuck the United States.*

He walked out to the street.

*Where's my ride, dammit?* He fidgeted, waiting at curbside, standing in the light rain, watching for the limo from the Chinese Embassy. He saw a man coming down the sidewalk with an umbrella. *I should have grabbed mine... stupid rain.*

The rumble of the big express bus rolling down the street captured his attention as it sped along in the curb lane. *Shit... damn bus*, he thought. The Director didn't want to get splashed by the bus passing down the wet street. Water was already puddling in the gutters and potholes. Stepping back, he felt an unexpected flat palm between his shoulder blades. A push... he fell forward into the street.

Bus driver Harold Johnson was focused on the rear-view mirror, eyeballing the hot chick in a mini skirt sitting awkwardly with knees apart in the side row. Typical of many young professional women, she dressed like she was heading for a night club than an office environment, her clothes revealing extensive cleavage and legs, yet she walked and sat with all the grace of a buggered kangaroo

*Oh yeah... she's fine... real fine.* Harold was in a good mood. He been accident free for six months this time and would soon be released from his disciplinary probation. He cruised along in his sixty-foot 2007 Flyer Industries transit bus, happily enjoying erotic thoughts about his comely passenger, squirming in his seat as he became physically aroused by his fantasy.

Then it happened.

Thump… a pause… thump, thump…

*Shit. All three axle\]s.*

Although he barely felt the body squish under his wheels, he cringed, knowing intuitively what just occurred, dammit… *why did that asshole have to fall in front of my bus?*

On the sidewalk, Kang the assassin smiled and walked away, the blue umbrella concealing his face as he disappeared around the corner into the alley where he parked his car. It was a shame to kill such a high-level asset, but they had so many in Washington, Chinese intelligence would hardly notice the loss.

Now it was time to disappear for a while… perhaps next year he would return to Washington and resume his professional practice of staging suicides.

As he approached his rental car, a tall Anglo woman, maybe Hispanic, possibly Italian, walked towards him with her head down, holding a leather notebook over her hair.

*Harmless.*

Kang continued ignoring her as he walked with purpose towards the sedan. Suddenly, he learned what it feels like when a United States Marine Corps fighting knife slips in between your ribs and rips your heart in half.

His body fell limp face-down on the damp pavement in a puddle of street filth and blood.

Erika Falcone smiled.

## MIAMI, FLORIDA

From the moment he heard about The FBI Director's death three days prior, Clammer knew his time was short. It must be the President behind this, he thought as he took the elevator to the roof of the towering high-rise hotel. That orange bastard can't play by the rules… and he never quits… bastard!

The CIA Director's rage at POTUS, the first elected official to not bow to his direction, infuriated him to the point of having a stroke. His temples uncontrollably pulsed with blood making him dizzy. But soon he would be aboard the charter helicopter taking him to Havana where he would be an honored guest of the Cuban government and a cooperating intelligence source for Castro's DGI. He could no longer trust the Chinese and all his rich and famous tech buddies were either dead or in hiding. No more good options were available. Cuba was his last best hope.

He stepped out of the elevator onto the roof, surprised to see the chartered helicopter was not on the pad waiting for him. Instead of a private helicopter service, he saw a man dressed in a black suit… an exceptionally large man, a cruel man, a violent man.

Clammer fought back panic. *What the hell? No!* Clammer knew this was bad. There was no charter helicopter coming. He ran back toward the elevator, but the door closed as he approached. With desperation, he repeatedly jammed his finger into the elevator button until he felt a big gloved hand grab him by the scruff of the neck and spin him around. The air exploded out of his lungs as the man slammed him against the wall.

He stared into the face of murder. He knew now that the abyss had finally come looking for him. His mind analyzed the scene… *the gray blue eyes of a killer… piercing and cruel. Long black hair and a bushy beard… a monster. barely human…* Clammer's mental assessment gave him only one word… *death.* Before him stood a man of violence.

Fraught with terror, the CIA Director reached for his weapon, but the man yanked the tiny revolver out of Clammer's holster first and slapped him across the face with his own gun, breaking some teeth and splitting his cheek with a deep six-inch cut.

The Director felt his knees involuntarily failing him, shaking with fear as thick warm blood ran down his face and neck.

The man spoke ominously, "You ordered the death of a good man. A patriotic American."

The smug and arrogant official whose inner-circle of subordinates revered like a monarch, chattered like an irate zoo monkey squeezing a handful of wet poop in its fist. "No, I didn't. Who are you? Why are you doing this? I'm the head of the CIA. You can't do this to me."

The man didn't respond. He delivered a brutal elbow to Clammer's solar plexus.

"How about that? Can I do *that* to you?"

The CIA Director collapsed on the concrete roof, shaking and sucking for air. "Why? Why are you doing this?"

"Because he'd do it for me."

Mac hoisted the director by the hair and the belt and raised him like he was jerk-pressing a two-hundred-and-fifty- pound barbell.

Clammer yipped a whiny screech as the beastly man thrust him into the air, squinting as his beady eyes were exposed to the sun.

Mac dropped to one knee and slammed the traitor's body back-first across his thigh, snapping Clammer's spine like a two-cent chop stick.

Mac growled as he rolled the limp figure off his leg, "I really wanted to twist your head off, asshole, but I want you alive all the way to the street." Then he said the last words Clammer would ever hear. "This is for Pearson."

The helpless CIA Director couldn't fathom that this was really happening. After all these years, he never suspected there would be actual consequences for his actions. And now… he was about to die at the hands of a beast… a murdering brute… a madman.

Mac grabbed Clammer by one ankle and dragged him to the edge of the roof where he dropped kicked him off the side of the building. He didn't bother watching the traitor's quick trip down, but he heard the splat of the impact. Meh…

The nice clean kill. made him smile as he thought back on the many ass-chewings the old man delivered over excessive violence on these missions. This one is for you, sir. Nice, neat, and clean… No shit show this time.

McCartney pulled the prepared suicide note that Deeter had prepared for the occasion out of his inner suit coat pocket and placed it conspicuously under a stone-sized chip of broken concrete he found on the roof.

He heard the ding and swish of the opening door and got on the elevator. Payback complete.

## San Clemente, California

Popular writer and conservative blogger Mike Carnavach got up to walk his dog. It was the typical Southern California summer morning, damp air, bright sun, and pleasantly warm. As the big man stepped onto the front porch of his home, he saw a legal sized parcel. Weird, he thought.

Carnavach pulled the folding knife out of his pocket and opened it cautiously.

"What the hell?"

The parcel contained a detailed outline of a conspiracy between the CIA, the FBI, and China. The dossier was accompanied by a series of emails, text messages, other documentation, a photo of Clammer's suicide note, and his lengthy confession. Another page had a short message. *'You're welcome.'*

Carnavach smiled.

## Palm Beach, Florida – The President's Resort

The state visit by the President and Chairman of China's Communist party was a gala affair. A private meeting followed photographs and speeches as the two world leaders retired to the President's secure office.

The President took a seat behind his desk and Lu sat down in front of him in the finely adorned leather chairs provided for guests.

The President of the United States began the conversation speaking in the standard diplomatic jargon used during these kinds of state visits, "President Lu, thank you for coming to see us at my request. I have something I'd like to show you.

"Of course, Mister President. Thank you for your generosity and hospitality."

"It's my pleasure." He skipped further pleasantries and got to the point. "Here is my concern." The American President laid out ten pages of documentation revealing the key steps in the bioweapon treachery presented in analytical diagrams and photographs including dates, names, times and locations.

President Lu sat open mouthed as a drunk partygoer who got caught pissing in the kitchen sink. "This is not true. What is this nonsense."

The President's expression hardened. He'd negotiated with the tough guys his whole life, from the head of the steel workers union in New York City to the leader of North Korea. "We both know it is true. So just stop right there. I have enough evidence here to take you into custody for crimes against humanity."

"But…" President Lu struggled to form a sentence before the POTUS shut him down.

"No buts… here is how this goes down. Number one, you immediately and unequivocally forgive any debt your country has from loans to the United States."

"Absolutely not! I can't do…" His words were cut off again.

"Two, I want every spy you have in our country called back or I have my people whack them."

"What? Whack? What is this whack?"

"Kill the bastards."

"But…"

The President ignored the protest and relentlessly pressed forward. "Three, free Taiwan and declare it a sovereign country."

"That is just not…"

"Four, and this is important. I want Zhao publicly executed."

President Lu blustered. "This is ridiculous. These demands are outrageous. My military will crush you for these meaningless threats."

The president remained stone faced. He pulled a small plastic device from his desk drawer. "Do you see this, Lu?"

President Lu, somewhat perplexed, nodded in the affirmative, uncertain what technology the POTUS held.

"In anticipation of this meeting I ordered the full force of America's military directed at your country. We have a lot of nukes…. So many nukes… more than anybody… the very best nukes. Enough to blow up the world ten times… And each and every one of them is pointed at your country right now. Our submarines have locked a firing solution on every navy vessel you have. Every so-called business executive you have working overseas has a Delta Operator nearby waiting for the signal to take them out… Let's be honest, your businessmen are military targets, aren't they? They're just weaponized assets acting at your government's direction against us."

"How can you dare say these words…"

The President proceeded with his diatribe, his voice lowering to a menacing snarl, "Every embassy you have in every country in the world is targeted from space with precision missiles. Every satellite you put in orbit is targeted and set for destruction." The President let the words sink in for a moment before continuing like a teacher explaining a simple task to a child, "I press the activator on this device, and every one of those weapons, and many more, will be immediately deployed. There will be no discussion, no war, no China… it will happen that fast. That I can tell you."

The blood drained from Lu's face. "You wouldn't do that." He nervously eyed the mysterious technology the President of the United States held partly concealed in his large hand.

The president smiled, "No, Lu… I really want to do this… I want to end your commie bullshit once and for all." The New York construction business attitude of the President began revealing itself. "I'm sick and tired of your bullying your neighbors, stealing our stuff, spying on our companies, and threatening world peace. You pay your agents in our media to rant about our pollution, but you are the world's worst polluter. Maybe the worst ever…Just horrible pollution. You menace, threaten, and intimidate the entire Pacific Rim with words of war while claiming peaceful intent… But in my role as the leader of the free world, and as our country is a beacon of hope for everyone, I have a moral obligation to at least *attempt* to protect your innocent citizens… if possible… and that obligation has now been met with this offer. I'm giving you only one opportunity to comply." He paused. "Now, I will drink a diet soda. When I'm done with it, if you haven't responded, you can kiss you country's ass goodbye and my men will come in here and arrest you… Got it, Lu Lu?" The President opened his soda with one hand and kept the device in the closed palm of his other hand at eye level with Lu.

The persuasive strength of this power move was unconventional but effective.

The President of China shook with rage. But he considered every report that Chinese intelligence analyzed from American media sources and spies. All of the sources agreed that the man sitting before him was simply crazy enough to do something like this. The man loved winning and he was capable of anything. He didn't care about diplomatic rules. He only cared about America.

Lu spoke, "What you propose will be the end of China as we know it."

"No… It will be a new beginning for China… Together your people and the American people will make China great again... mainly by getting rid of you commie bastards and us setting your people free… But it will be hard work. Very hard. So please, Lu… be an asshole and let me activate this device. I'd like nothing better than to end this right now."

A humbled Lu hung his head in defeat. "We will comply."

The President smiled and stood, towering over the smaller man. "Why don't you get with your people and when you're done, we can join the others. I'll be here waiting for confirmation."

Lu got up from his chair, head hanging. With his chin resting on his chest, he skulked out of the office, dejected, humiliated, and crushed. The techno-war lost. The communist era of China was at an end.

The President of the United States returned his youngest son's fidget spinner to the drawer, leaned back in his chair, and thought up a new nickname for the leader of China. "Little LuLu..." he chuckled.

# Epilogue

The President of the United States sipped a bottled water as he drove his top-of-the-line electric golf cart across the sprawling resort estate. He noticed a member of the Secret Service detail nearby animatedly chattering on the radio.

The agent hopped off the golf cart and sprinted over to the President. "Sir, we have a priority message."

"What is it?" POTUS asked.

The grim agent announced, "I'm sorry to have to inform you of this, Mister President, so soon after the tragic news about the FBI Director, but the Director of the has CIA committed suicide. He jumped from the top of a Miami skyscraper and fell to his death. Director Clammer is dead."

The President shrugged. "That's too bad." He took another sip from the bottled water. "But hey, if you happen to have a resume handy, it sounds like we have a some new job openings in federal law enforcement now if you're interested."

The agent tried to suppress a smile, knowing there was no love lost between the President and the Director... or CIA Officers and the Director... or federal law enforcement and the Director. In her experience as a Secret Service Agent, she didn't see the CIA Director often, but she thought he always came off as being a smug yet incompetent political dickhead. The FBI director had been cut from the same cloth. To be fair, the President could be a bit of an asshole too on occasion, but at least he was honest, fun, authentic, and in the job for all the right reasons... a substantial and refreshing change from most of the jerks she had protected in the line of duty over the years. And, like the Secret Service, this President got the job done at all costs. He treated his position like sacred duty rather than as an all-access taxpayer-funded pass. POTUS refused to be bullied around by the eternal bureaucrat class like the others before him. "No thank you, Mister President. I'd prefer to stick with you, if you don't mind."

The President responded with a roguish smile, "I could go for a burger. How about you?"

"Sounds good, sir."

The President grinned. "Last one to the Ocean Grill buys." He sped away in his golf cart with his security detail in close pursuit.

## CORONADO, CALIFORNIA

Mac stretched out on his beach chair with a margarita concealed in a stainless-steel mug. He had a gallon sized thermos of them for backup. Plugging the earphones of his MP3 player in his ears he tuned in some tropical tunes… steel drum music, Key West favorites, a little Reggae. Life is good.

To his left was the Hotel Del Coronado. To his right was North Island Naval Air Station. In front of him was the Pacific Ocean. He could see US Navy warships doing Navy shit miles off the coast and a flotilla of recreational sailboats doing sailboat shit near the group of islands to the south in Mexican waters.

He raised his drink to the setting sun.

"To absent companions… Thank you, sir…I will never forget you, Mister Pearson. Rest easy soldier. We got this now."

His cell phone vibrated interrupting the moment. He looked down at it and saw Deeter's number on the screen. Mac took the call. "Yeah?" he answered vaguely.

The President's son skipped pleasantries and asked. "Have you been to Venezuela lately?

"No…"

"We have a matter of some urgency there that requires your assistance. Falcone is on the way. She was already in the neighborhood anyway. Can you roll?"

Mac quoted one of America's greatest heroes, "Let's roll." He smiled. He took one more drink before gathering his beach chair and cooler. *What a great country.*

*The end*

## About Bronco Hammer - Author

Bronco Hammer, a native son of Texas, currently resides in Coronado, California. Hammer spends most of time aboard his boat, the Wandering Star, which is docked at a secret location somewhere near the Mexican border.

He can often be found at various happy hours on the island. His interests include trucks, boats, horses, beer, guns, and science.

Above is the only known photograph of Hammer. It is believed by some to have been taken in Czechoslovakia in 1990.

*Stay in touch at broncohammer.com*

## About Dan, Senior Creative Consultant

After retiring from a twenty-three-year law enforcement career, Dan focused his attention on various endeavors that remain classified to this day, mainly because he forgot most of them. Now, he works as an advisor to the most dangerous writer in the world and hangs out at the beach enjoying cocktails and sunsets.

In addition to his duties as a beach bum, he spends quite a bit of his time attempting to prevent Bronco Hammer from drinking all his beer.

Made in the USA
Monee, IL
16 March 2020